KV-638-733

JUSTICE IN THE SADDLE

JUSTICE IN THE SADDLE

by

Logan Stuart

Dales Large Print Books
Long Preston, North Yorkshire,
BD23 4ND, England.

British Library Cataloguing in Publication Data.

Stuart, Logan
    Justice in the saddle.

    A catalogue record of this book is
    available from the British Library

    ISBN   1-84262-118-1 pbk

First published in Great Britain in 1954 by Rich & Cowan

Cover illus   rrangement with
Alison Eldr

The moral   asserted

Published i   ement with
Roxy Bellaı

All Rights   ı publication may be
reproduced, stored in a retrieval system, or transmitted in any
form or by any means, electronic, mechanical, photocopying,
recording or otherwise without the prior permission of the
Copyright owner.

Dales Large Print is an imprint of Library Magna Books Ltd.

Printed and bound in Great Britain by
T.J. (International) Ltd., Cornwall, PL28 8RW

Cecil P Malley, FRCS

CONTENTS

CHAPTER 1

A LETTER FROM PAULA

Will Kermody's high figure was slouched in the saddle, his down-bent head seemingly butting the hard, driving rain. Light from the nearest of the town buildings shone on the streaming slicker as the man moved his body uncomfortably on wet leather.

He brought his gaze up now, peering through the darkness and the rain, orientating himself to Selwyn's Main Street and the familiar buildings at this end of the town.

He speculated again, as he had done all along the four-mile ride, with a coldly analytical quality, as to why he had turned out from the warmth and comparative comfort of the Stirrup bunkhouse on a night like this.

Usually, Will Kermody was too busy to feel any sort of loneliness, but tonight, somehow or another, the unfamiliar feeling had come upon him and had refused to budge.

The late spring rainstorm, however, had not been sufficient to dampen the spirits of

11

most of Stirrup's riders, and earlier on in the evening those free of chores had saddled up and ridden to town for a mild Saturday-night carousal.

Phil Hankins, the *segundo*, had gone and so had Sid Vincent and Dave Swallow. Jim Stewart and Fay Murphy were line-riding at Stirrup's eastern line-cabin and that left Brecker Chase and Chuck Anderson, the cook, playing poker in the increasingly oppressive and sweaty atmosphere of the bunk-house.

Will was feeling the strain of long hours in the saddle. For the past week he had ridden farther and for more continuous hours than any other of the crew. Spring round-up was a gruelling time at best and, until yesterday, the weather had been unusually hot and dry.

But late rain, coming down Pilgrim Valley in bucketfuls Friday night and most of Saturday, had put a temporary brake on the business of rounding up three-year-olds for the trail; branding and ear-marking calves and dividing mavericks fairly between Ward Cabot's Stirrup and Mike Lannigan's Slash M and Ed Narroway's Circle D.

Thus the three neighbouring spreads mutually agreed to call a halt to the work for the time being, and as everyone had sweated blood and they were well up to schedule with their tallies, the decision was easily made.

Will had stretched himself out on his bunk, rolling and lighting a cigarette and idly listening for the sounds from the adjoining cook-shack which would tell him that Chuck was ready with the evening meal.

But this restless, lonely mood had crawled in from somewhere and had settled on Will Kermody like some blood-sucking parasite that would not be shifted.

Before even the triangle sent out its harsh clanging summons, Will had pulled on boots, slicker and hat and had pushed out into the pelting rain of the late afternoon, saddling his own roan-and-white pony in a mood of almost angry desperation.

Perhaps, he figured, he needed a trip to town. A drink might do no harm and he could eat at Chung Lee's or Pilgrim House. Will had mounted the steps of the ranch-house, glimpsing through the screen-doors the burly figure of Ward Cabot, owner of the Stirrup spread.

'Riding into town, Ward,' Will said, unfastening the door and leaning his high, slickered figure against the jamb.

Cabot nodded, understanding this taciturn foreman of his better than most; appreciating, too, the qualities that made this man a top hand even over a first-class crew such as Stirrup's.

'Who's down at the bunk-house, Will?'

13

Cabot said practically.

'Brec and Chuck. Phil took the rest to town earlier.'

Ward nodded. There was the merest sliver of anxiety in his next words.

'You won't stay overnight?'

Will grinned without mirth and slowly shook his head.

'I'll see the boys are back before midnight, Ward. If this rain clears tonight we'll be up to an early start tomorrow even it if is Sunday.'

Ward Cabot lifted his hand in casual salute as Will turned to go. 'You do what you think best, Will,' he said as Kermody's dark, rain-slashed figure found leather in the wet-running gloom.

So Will had started off for town, pushed by this crowding feeling of loneliness or frustration, or maybe just over-tiredness.

But Kermody grinned bleakly as he rode, rejecting the thought, now that the cool dissecting mind had had time to work, that this mood had anything to do with fatigue or frustration.

He bent his head to the wind and rain, feeling the water pour off the brim of his wide, low-crowned stetson, and seeing through the beating weather the lovely face of Paula Cabot, as he always saw it when this feeling crept up on him.

Paula Mackinnon, he corrected himself

bitterly. Paula Mackinnon she had been ever since last spring, and perhaps that was why, now that winter had come and gone, he was feeling the tugging of long-buried emotions.

At least they *should* have been long buried, Will reminded himself, but at such times as these they had the habit of rising to confront him, like disembodied spirits, refusing to be shut out by the hard wall of his resolve.

He felt the gelding stumble slightly in a water-filled rut, and automatically sawed on the reins, at the same time pulling hard on his thoughts and peering ahead along the trail where the distant rain-blurred lights of Selwyn winked like bubbles of light on a phosphorescent sea.

Will made straight for the livery, mildly observing that a few riders had left their saddle-mounts tied to racks along the soaking street. And for all the weather, Selwyn was beginning to get under way with its Saturday-night 'shivareeing'.

Pete Jansen, the hostler, moved out of the doorway as Will brought in the Stirrup pony.

'Nice night, Will,' Jansen grunted. 'Reckon maybe there's rain about.'

Will smiled and for the first time felt this strange mood of his slacken its grip.

'Sure, Pete. Stirrup behaving itself to-night?'

Jansen caught up a lighted storm lantern and preceded Will and his mount to a vacant stall.

'So far,' the old man grunted, 'Phil's kinda holdin' them on a tight reign, I guess. They's over to the Palace Saloon right now.'

Will nodded, shucking out of his slicker and hanging it on a peg on the wall.

Pete watched while the Stirrup ramrod adjusted the shell-belt around his lean hips and settled the holstered Colt at his right leg.

Then the two men leisured their way back to the wide entrance of the livery, on one side of which was Pete Jansen's office.

Will rolled a cigarette and reached in his shirt pocket for a match. He exploded the sulphur end with his thumb-nail and set the light to his quirly, nodding to the hostler as he made to ascend the nearby board-walk.

'Hey, wait a minute, Will! Jest remembered the sheriff was askin' if you'd bin around. Reckon he wants to see you–'

'On what charge?' Will Kermody grinned.

Pete Jansen gave his throaty chuckle. His fat face wobbled as he joined in the joke.

'You cain't imagine Herb Wilson arresting anyone, can you, Will?'

Kermody thought for a moment of the mild-mannered, quiet-voiced sheriff of Selwyn, mentally siding with the hostler at first in his summing up of Herb Wilson, and

16

then presently rejecting this whole-hearted agreement. More than once Will Kermody had seen the hard core of Herb Wilson's resolve emerge from the soft outer shell of the man. Perhaps he knew Herb better even than Pete knew him.

'Wal, I dunno even as how he wanted to see you special, Will,' Jansen rumbled. 'Jest drifted along an' asked if you'd bin around.'

Will nodded his thanks and crossed the muddy street, making first for Chung Lee's place and suddenly changing his mind in mid-stride and fetching up outside Pilgrim House, Selwyn's one hotel.

Under the shelter of the roofed-in board-walk, Will removed his hat, swinging it downwards, hard, to remove the worst of the rain which had collected during his brief walk across the street.

Lights from Pilgrim House and one or two nearby stores and saloons momentarily limned the Stirrup ramrod in their rays, revealing the dark, flat-planed face, the longish red-brown hair and the rather surprisingly paler eyebrows, bleached light by the many summer suns of Pilgrim Valley. At the moment, in the sharp contrast between light and shadow, Will's keen grey eyes seemed black. It was only for a moment he stood thus, as men shouldered by him along the plank-walk, some nodding a sober greeting, others indulging in some witticism about the weather. Then, abruptly, he swung into the hotel, pausing a moment to accustom his eyes to the brighter lights inside and then heading towards the velvet drapes on the right of the desk, beyond which was situated the bar.

Will nodded to men he knew – townsfolk, a few punchers – and called for whisky. He felt the air around him damp and oppressive, charged with the unmistakable, and slightly offensive, smell of damp garments drying on damp bodies.

There was no sign of Kermody's particular friends, Ed Narroway or Mike Lannigan, and Will downed another drink and turned on his heel, shouldering past the drapes and selecting a cigar from the stand close to the desk. He threw a coin on to the counter, exchanging a brief pleasantry with Omar Werner, the hotel's clerk, and crossed the lobby to the restaurant.

It was not surprising that the tables were crowded. This was Saturday night and folk were out to enjoy themselves. A meal out, a few drinks and maybe an all-night poker session at back of one of the stores. For the younger bloods and one or two miners from Clear Fork it would be the Palace Saloon with its monte, faro and roulette lay-out. The percentage girls were an additional attraction to most of the single men – and some of the married ones!

Will's gazed moved over the heads of folk busy eating and switched to his 'own' table; one that was usually reserved for him if Becky Laas, the waitress, expected him.

Tonight there was a woman sitting there with her back to the door, but there were still two vacant places and this was still the least crowded of the tables.

Kermody threaded a way through the restaurant, drew out a chair and murmured an apology, addressing the sleek top of the down-bent head.

The girl looked up quickly, pleasure lighting her face and making it almost beautiful.

If Will had realized it had been Celia Owen sitting there he might have waited for another table, but it was too late now to draw back.

He sat down at the girl's warm invitation, drawing on the cigar and then stubbing it out as the smoke drifted across to her nostrils, causing her to swallow hard; the blue-grey eyes to water.

'I'm sorry,' Will smiled, laying the cigar down. 'I guess it doesn't go with eating, anyway.'

Becky came up, patting her hair in the eternal gesture, and wetting the tip of her pencil with a pink tongue. Will smiled inwardly at this routine which was always the same with Becky Laas and gave his order.

19

Celia drew her coffee-cup forward and stirred vigorously.

'How's the dress-shop going, Celia; getting plenty of orders?'

The girl sipped her coffee, considering the question, and her answer, carefully. She was too proud to ask for or take any help even though she knew that Will Kermody would willingly stake her if he knew how tough things were. Yet, Celia Owen was almost too honest to lie and say everything was fine. She brushed the question aside, switching attention from herself to the man with characteristic feminine technique.

'All right, Will. How are things with you? We haven't seen you in town for over a week!'

Kermody smiled almost deprecatingly, giving to his hardlined, brash face a rare softness of which he was entirely unaware.

'Don't reckon you've seen Mike, either, Celia–'

'Lannigan?' Celia Owen's lip curled. 'He's so – so uncouth, and he – well, *why* haven't either of you been around?'

'Round-up,' Will said succinctly, and made the arrival of his steak and fried potatoes an excuse for silence.

When he had finished the meal he re-lit the cigar and drank his coffee, his mind fingering Celia's earlier remarks; her tone of scathing contempt when referring to the boss of the small Slash M outfit.

Will thought suddenly that Selwyn's dressmaker needed a spanking and for a moment a wicked impulse nudged him, so that he half rose from the chair, until the more sober side of him restored the balance.

But Kermody finished the movement of rising to his feet and made his excuses to Celia, moving through the emptying restaurant with deceptively long strides.

The girl had not believed him, of course, when he had told her about seeing a man in town. It was just the usual brush-off. That's what Celia Owen would believe, and Will Kermody shrugged as his boots hit the board-walk with a resounding impact.

He stood a moment against the hotel veranda, gazing at the reflection of lights in the pools on Main, watching them break and shatter as riders and an occasional buggy or spring-wagon splashed through the puddles. Slowly the mud settled again and the winking lights came back. For a moment Will felt that there must be something symbolic in all this, but for the life of him he could not determine what it was.

His glance took in the weather again, as he noted the freshening breeze coming down from the snow-capped Spanish Peaks at this eastern end of Pilgrim Valley.

Already the rain was lessening perceptibly,

and if the wind held and perhaps veered a little southwards Will figured the late rains might finish suddenly.

He noted the light shining through the top half of the sheriff's office and recollected that Herb Wilson had enquired his whereabouts.

Now Kermody ducked under the rack in front of him, negotiating the sudden rush of evening traffic with a sixth sense and ascending the board-walk opposite.

He passed Sam Schmidt's general store, guessing at the poker game that was going on at back. Rip Prescott's barber-shop was next door, then Eli Warner's saddle-shop.

Will stepped down and across the alley separating the saddlery from the sheriff's office and jail, lifting the latch and pushing into the smoke-laden room.

Herb Wilson glanced up from his desk, removed his pipe to spit and said mildly, 'Howdy, Will.'

Kermody pushed back his hat and sank into a battered leather chair which received him with a series of protesting squeaks and creaks.

Wilson put down his pencil, swivelled his chair round so that he was facing the Stirrup ramrod.

Kermody noticed the piece of paper in his hand as Herb leaned forward, thrusting it at Will with his outstretched hand.

'A letter from Paula, Will. Read it.'

Kermody's questioning gaze at last dropped to the sheet of notepaper covered with Paula Mackinnon's unmistakable and flourishing writing.

Will threw the all but finished cigar into the brass cuspidor and slowly read the letter from start to finish. He looked up then, a puzzled expression creeping into his grey eyes, and Herb said quietly, 'Read it again, Will.'

This time the ramrod read the letter aloud.

> *'Golden Dollar Saloon,*
> *Clear Fork,*
> *Archer County.*
> *18th May, 1879*

Dear Herb

It seems such a long time ago that I left Selwyn to come here with Ben, and yet in all that time I have neither written nor come to see you.

I feel very ashamed of myself but it is not because I have not wanted to, and tried – I mean Ben has been so busy here making money – yes, we're really doing fine, except that I don't get out much and could use a few good friends like you and Will.

I would dearly like to see Dad but Ben will not let – I mean Ben figures I am being useful to him right here by his side.

I am in good health and, except for a silly eye

which keeps on watering, feeling fine.

Do send me news of yourself and the others in the valley – Will, Ed, Doris Schmidt, Celia, Mike, but please address the note to Laura Paramour at this address. She is a very good friend of mine and Ben might perhaps feel jealous if I had a letter from Selwyn. One or two that have come by stage, from Celia and Doris, have been destroyed before I could read them.

I am giving this note to Jack Taylor the stage-driver and know you will receive it.

Much love to you, Herb, and all at Stirrup.

Paula.'

Will replaced the letter in Herb Wilson's hand, feeling a sudden upsurge of raw anger.

When Kermody spoke his voice was barely controlled. 'I always figured Ben Mackinnon was a swine, Herb. Not because I was the unlucky man, but–'

The sheriff nodded and laid his pale grey gaze on the ramrod's face. 'That's the way I figger et, Will. Paula's tryin' to cover up, but my guess is Ben's giving her a rough time. Did you ever hear Paula Cabot talk about bein' in "good health"? 'Course she was allus in good health, so there was no reason to mention it!

'That bit about the letter, too, and sendin' a reply to Laura Paramour–'

Will's gaze was bleak as it moved over the

sheriff opposite.

'There's one-two smudges on the ink, Herb, like she might have been crying. That's why she mentioned about her bad eye!'

'What you figger on doin', Will?' Herb asked softly.

'Goddammit to hell!' Kermody snarled, rising to his feet and pacing the office. 'A man can't ride over to Clear Fork and shoot down Ben Mackinnon because he figures Ben's giving his wife a raw deal–'

'I doubt if my badge would be big enough if you did, Will,' the sheriff said quietly. 'It makes it doubly worse, seein' that some folks know you're still in love with Paula…'

Will Kermody stood still. 'There must be a way, Herb, to even things up with Ben. To leave Paula free–'

'I reckon there is,' Herb said mildly, and for a moment Kermody missed the import of the sheriff's softly spoken remark.

Will reached for his makings, shaping a cigarette with exquisite care, the better to get his feelings under control.

Presently he lit the cigarette and said, 'You got any ideas, Herb?'

Sheriff Wilson's long-horn moustaches twitched as his lips moved in a wintry smile. The rain-grey eyes were expressionless.

'You noticed any rustlin' goin' on in the valley lately, Will?'

'You mean on Stirrup range?'

'Stirrup, Slash M, Circle D, any of 'em.'

'Why, Herb, it's early in the year yet. None of us have completed our tally. As far as Stirrup's concerned we wouldn't know, I guess, if a few head were moved off quietly now and again. But as for Mike Lannigan and Ed Narroway, they only run a few hundred head. Maybe they'd know more quickly than Stirrup if they had any losses. Why, Herb? What's this leading to?'

This time there was a little warmth in Sheriff Wilson's smile. His hand made a rasping noise as he drew it along his stubbled jaw in a slow, thoughtful gesture.

'Jack Taylor was tellin' me about a hide he'd seen half buried jest outside Clear Fork. Leastways et had bin buried proper, no doubt, but the rain had kinda disturbed et. Jack wuz curious an' stopped the coach, seein' there wuz only him an' Pete Watkins the guard, and a drummer inside.'

'Go on, Herb.'

Sheriff Wilson nodded. 'Jack's a good man, Will, you know. He figgered I might be interested as well as Lannigan and you–'

'Whose brand, Herb?'

Wilson grinned now. At last Will Kermody had arrived.

'The fust one was Slash M–'

'The *first* one?'

'Sure! Jack nosed around and found

26

another hide. He cut out the brands on both of 'em. Look, son!'

Wilson unlocked and opened a drawer in his desk as he spoke and withdrew two pieces of roughly cut, hairy hide, holding them out for the Stirrup man's closer inspection.

In spite of the winter hair, it was fairly easy to see last fall's brand-marks. The Slash M was faint, but the Stirrup brand showed more clearly.

'Someone's sneakin' a few head at a time to feed the miners in Clear Fork, or else selling the butchered meat some place else. Soon they'll be cuttin' out a sizeable herd–'

'Who? Do you know who?'

'Wal,' Herb drawled, 'ef et ain't Ben Mackinnon, I don't see why we shouldn't fix et for him to take the rap!'

Kermody slowly relaxed as he exhaled twin streamers of smoke from his nostrils.

'He's guilty of wife-beating, Herb,' Will said thinly. 'He can't be brought to book for that, but he can for rustling–'

Sheriff Wilson nodded gently. His face was placid, his smile benign.

CHAPTER 2

'I'LL SIDE YOU, WILL!'

'Do you want fer the boys to git on brandin' those strays we corralled over to red bluffs, Will?' Phil Hankins drawled.

It was significant that the *segundo* could suggest such work to Will Kermody even on a Sunday, in the full knowledge that the men would be willing, with good-natured grumbling, if Will thought such work was necessary.

The two men leaned against the pole corral in the early light of Sunday morning, watching young Tim Furnival turn the *remuda* into the corral.

Will's glance was on the slow-moving sails of the windmill. As he had hoped, the wind had veered south-east and had then remained steady. The rain had cleared last night, and although the ground was soggy and ruts were filled with water, there was the promise of good early summer weather ahead.

The clean, rain-washed air filled Kermody's nostrils and the smell of leather and horses was a crowding but pleasant odour.

Intermingled with these smells was the heady scent of fresh young sage, blown across the range by the gently rippling breeze.

Will's thoughts had been on his talk with Sheriff Wilson last night. The anger against Ben Mackinnon burned in him just as strongly this morning, but the first rough shock of it had become burnished smooth by a cold, implacable determination.

He dragged his thoughts back to Phil's words as he weighed the prospect of lighting branding fires out on the range with soaking greasewood and sage-brush.

Will said: 'They might as well look to ropes, bridles and cinch-straps today, Phil. For what we should get done I don't figure it's worth it.

'I'm riding over to Slash M this morning. I can tell Lannigan we'll start in tomorrow.'

Phil nodded and grinned. 'Birdie' – that was Dave Swallow – 'was sure hopin' you'd figger et thetaway, Will. He's got a hangover big as Spanish Peaks!'

'He shouldn' drink Burr Corrigan's rot-gut at the Palace,' Will said, pushing away from the pole-fence and walking towards the gate.

His saddle complete with lariat was across the top-bar and casually and easily Will built his loop and paid out the rope, whirling it low and then higher, gauging his distance and the speed of the now running, twisting ponies.

The noose settled over the roan-and-white gelding's head and the beast came forward as Will gently pulled on the rope.

He threw blanket and saddle across its back and drew the bridle swiftly over its head. The whole operation had taken a bare three minutes.

Phil nodded his admiration. He couldn't help it. It was always the same when Kermody went into action. He appeared almost slow at times, yet when other hands were still buckling cinch-straps or fumbling with bridles, Will was most always already mounted and waiting.

Kermody lifted a hand to the *segundo*. 'Tell Ward where I'm going, Phil,' he called, and put the gelding west towards Cedar Creek, a creek of the Pilgrim and the boundary between Stirrup and Slash M.

All this side of the valley belonged to Stirrup, both north and south of the river, but west of Cedar Fork was Slash M, Circle D and a scattering of small homesteaders, mostly out-of-pants, who clung to a precarious existence through the tolerance of Ed Narroway and Mike Lannigan.

Will gave the roan-and-white its head until the animal had let off its exuberant spirits. The ramrod's gaze lifted to the snow-tipped Spanish Peaks and travelled around in an arc across the lush range, and on to the distant foothills of the Goya range on whose talus slopes the mining camp-cum-town of Clear Fork was precariously perched.

He thought again of Paula's letter, realizing that although there was no proof of Ben's mis-treatment of her, it bore out what both he and Herb Wilson had thought ever since Paula had married the dashing and handsome Mackinnon with his sweeping cavalry moustaches and his hell-for-leather air.

The fact that Paula must quickly have realized her mistake made things no better. Only worse, because Paula Cabot, Will figured, was a woman who would bear whatever cross was loaded upon her slim shoulders, if for no other reason than through a fierce, almost unreasoning sense of loyalty.

Kermody shook his head. No! He couldn't see Paula running out on Ben, even if there were just cause and even though Ward would be brim-full of delight to have her back at Stirrup. Paula may be headstrong, a little wild perhaps, and young enough to be seduced by qualities in men like Mackinnon that a more mature woman would see through. But whatever her faults, Will Kermody knew that she was loyal to the point of obstinacy, and that once she had set her feet along a certain path, that fierce single-mindedness of purpose, or obstinacy, coupled with pride that would never let her admit the going was rough – those qualities, Will thought, would bind her to Ben's side more strongly than any rawhide thongs!

It meant, then, that if Paula were to be saved from a life of misery – Mackinnon's small sadistic cruelties, his unreasoning jealousy and his supremely hateful egotism – then something would have to be accomplished in spite of the girl herself.

Will thought of Herb Wilson's plan as he put the Stirrup pony to the fording place at Cedar Creek, subconsciously noting how full the water ran after the heavy rains...

It was nearing noon when he looked down on the small, insignificant buildings of Slash M, but there was no trace of a sneer on Will's broad lips.

Mike Lannigan had come to Pilgrim Valley a bare three years ago, virtually penniless. With his own hands he had built the ranch-house from unpeeled firs which he had cut and hauled from further up the lower slopes of Spanish Peaks.

Kermody and Ward Cabot, when they had discovered this, had sent help, and in no time at all the cabin had sprung up, with a dutch barn and small stable and outhouses adjoining.

Mike had been eternally grateful. He had spent his last dollar filing on his unclaimed strip of land and buying it together with a few cows and one or two beef critturs.

Ward, on seeing this, had talked with Will and together they had cut out and driven over a herd of twenty-five prime steers including over a dozen cow critturs.

'Five dollars a head, Mike, and you can pay us when you're on your feet,' Ward had said gruffly.

Mike had just stood and stared, un-ashamedly blinking back tears and looking as though God had spoken to him.

There was nothing Lannigan would not do for Will Kermody or the Cabots. He was a man whose gratitude and remembrances grew rather than diminished with the pass-age of time.

Fred Robards ambled round the side of the house, putting his rheumy gaze to the rider approaching the yard. The oldster recognized the pony first and waved a hand.

Mike appeared in the entrance of the ranch-house.

'Hullo, Will,' he grinned. 'Light down and have some coffee!'

Will nodded and swung himself from leather, while Robards hitched the gelding's reins to the rack out front.

The ranch-house, small though it was, had a veranda on two sides, and now Will sank into a wooden rocker, while Mike Lannigan disappeared inside the house to fetch coffee.

He came out a few minutes later and Will covertly studied the chunky Slash M owner. He was little more than middle height but powerfully built, barrel-chested, with wide shoulders sloping down to muscular arms. Underneath the thin, work-stained Levi's Will could see the corded muscles of the man's thighs and lower legs as he moved in his chair.

Will lit a cigarette and tossed the sack into Mike's lap. Without preamble he drew out the two pieces of roughly hacked hide which Herb Wilson had loaned him last night, and threw them on the table in front of him. He drank some of the java, his eyes watching Mike Lannigan's red, blocky face.

Mike picked them up gingerly at first. Then his puzzled eyes spotted the brands. First Stirrup and then, more faintly on the other one, Slash M.

Lannigan leaped at it quickly enough. 'Rustled beef, Will?'

Kermody nodded. 'Found near Clear Fork. Someone's been running a few of our steers over there, Mike, and butchering them quietly and selling the beef to the miners or some other willing buyer–'

'My god, Will. I cain't afford to lose stock, even in ones or twos. Slash M's not big enough for that. Besides, this thing might grow if we've got rustlers in the valley!'

Will nodded. 'But it won't grow, Mike.

34

We'll see to that.'

'How?'

'By moving against a certain person in Clear Fork. Whether he's guilty of this I don't know. I don't care. He's sure got a lot to answer for in respect of his wife.'

Mike's brows drew together.

'I don't follow, Will.'

Will Kermody leaned back and gave the Slash M owner a brief word-picture of what had happened last night in the sheriff's office.

Lannigan's red face was dark and anger-splotched when Will had finished.

'You're sure about this, I mean the letter, Will? There couldn't be any mistake–?'

Kermody said bleakly: 'No mistake, Mike. Herb Wilson's shown us a way to sic the law on that bustard. We can't touch him for wife-beating but we *can* fix him for cattle-stealing! Seeing that someone's taken at least one Slash M steer and inasmuch as you've always thought a helluva lot of Paula, I figured you might want in on this!'

Mike's blue eyes burned brightly. 'I'll side you, Will! Guess there ain't no one could stop me. What do we do?'

Kermody considered a moment.

'It's a long pull to Clear Fork. If we start this afternoon we'll make it by tomorrow morning. Mackinnon's got a ranch of sorts, nearby. Maybe we can find him there. We'll nose around some and see if we can pick up any sign.

'Meanwhile you'll have to leave your count in Robard's hands and I'll have to let Phil Hankins and Ward know what I'm doing.'

Lannigan nodded. 'I'll fix this end of it, Will. Where and when shall I meet you?'

'Meet me late afternoon where that stand of willows runs down to Cedar Fork on your side. You know?'

Lannigan nodded. 'Sure. I'll be there, Will. *With a gun!*'

It seemed to Will that the golden disc of the sun was balancing itself on the peaks of the Goya range to the west. These mountains, unlike Spanish Peaks to the north, were not so towering or impressive. But on their topmost peaks, winter snow still lingered, reluctant to melt and swell the rushing mountain streams.

Now the lowering sun spread its red-gold halation over the blue-white heights, setting the mountain tops alight and sliding fingers of rich orange and flame down the south-western slopes, so that for a moment it seemed to Will that the Goya range was volcanic and that burning lava was flowing slowly down the sides.

He grinned to himself at his flights of fancy and the roan-and-white pony laid back its ears and blew down its nose, and Will's hand dropped easily to his thigh, inches only from the butt of his Colt.

He heard the rider approaching further down at the edge of the brakes and followed his route by carefully listening to the direction of the sounds.

In a few moments Will saw him threading through the willows, recognizing the chunky figure of Mike in the saddle of a Slash M pony.

Will raised his arm and neck-reined his mount, joining up with Lannigan with no more than a nod and a brief word of greeting. This was going to be no social visit!

They struck out cross-country at first, planning to hit the stage-road later on.

Firstly it was quicker across the range and secondly they were not anxious to meet chance travellers, not even the stage which made the journey twice a week, completing each trip in a day by driving hard and changing teams at Zach Keeler's half-way trading post.

Dusk was enjoying its brief short-lived reign when Lannigan broke the silence with a question. Will said: 'I'm not sure where Mackinnon's ranch is, Mike, but from what I've heard it's over the other side of Clear Fork. That means we can ask in town first thing in the morning.'

Lannigan nodded and murmured half

apologetically: 'I've bin thinkin', Will. Even if we brace Mackinnon we shore won't get much out of him from what I've heard. S'posin' we stick around in town fust, maybe we kin pick up a lead. Then, whether we do or not, we kin still go on to Ben's ranch later in the evening.'

Kermody examined the suggestion carefully and found it as good as any plan that had shaped itself in his own mind.

They made a dry night-camp when they were still some three-four miles from the stage-trail and another ten from Clear Fork.

Well before dawn both men were out of their blankets, hunkered down before a cheery fire, munching dried meat and waiting for steam to set the lid of the coffee-pot jumping.

'You haven't bin to Clear Fork in recent months, Will?' Mike said presently, setting the two tin mugs on a flat stone close to the fire.

'No,' Kermody said slowly. 'Not since – not since Paula married and went there.'

Will wondered at his own restraint in this matter. Many times during the summer and fall months of last year he had felt an almost irresistible urge to ride out, just for one glance at Paula's face. Just to have one word with her and to see for himself that she was all right. That was what he told himself, that it would be for a quick reassuring look. But he knew that there was every possibility that old wounds would be opened and feelings that he had kept hog-tied might quite well break through the self-imposed bonds of his resolve.

There was another point, too – perhaps more important – that was to do with Paula's own position. A man did not usually go visiting a married woman, even if he were an old friend – not if the man was known to have been sweet on the girl before she married.

Will cared nothing for range talk or the cess-pool insinuations of a mining camp as far as he was concerned. But Paula deserved something more than being tagged with such labels, and that would have happened, Kermody was sure.

Now, he was coming to Clear Fork at last, but on a different kind of errand. However he and Lannigan played this it would soon become known to everyone in Clear Fork that the Pilgrim Valley cattlemen were nosing around for 'stray' beef.

Will considered this aspect briefly and decided it might not be a bad thing. Even if it tipped their hand it might cause someone to act unwisely in sudden panic, leaving, perhaps, a clearer trail than if they just sat tight. He wondered again whether Ben really *did* have anything to do with this and hoped to God that it was so.

Kermody decided that he wouldn't mind Ben rustling a thousand head of Stirrup beef if only it could be proved and Mackinnon strung up to the nearest tall tree!...

Pearl grey and soft madder were fading in the eastern sky before the advent of cobalt and gold. In a little while the sun would be lifting above Selwyn at their backs.

They had a second cup of coffee and then kicked out the fire, saddling and unpicketing their mounts and swinging into leather.

They struck the stage trail before the sun was a half-hour old, and by the middle of the fore-noon were riding into Clear Fork's Main Street – it if could be so described.

There was every evidence to Will's eyes that here was another hell-roarin' mining camp and he remembered that yesterday was Sunday. There would be more than the usual quota of broken heads and damaged hands this morning, he figured, as both men put their gaze to the bottle- and refuse-littered street, the unpainted ramshackle buildings, the crazy board-walks which were no more than boards laid on flat stones over the muddy ground. Where the boards ended, folk of both sexes alike were forced to wade through the reddish, drying mud.

There were jostling men and women precariously edging their way along the plank-walks as though negotiating a particularly flimsy suspension bridge over a mighty river. Doors of saloons and stores – Will quickly counted five of the former – were open to the warm yet invigorating mountain air. On several vacant lots tents were pitched, outside of which were various crudely painted signs proclaiming the wares for sale or giving some particularly compelling reason why the inhabitants of Clear Fork should enter and sample the goods inside!

Between roughly constructed wooden saloons and stores and the temporarily erected tents were crude shacks, thrown up without thought or design, the main and indeed the only purpose being to shelter the occupant for the night.

Kermody's gaze laid itself along this street of indescribable filth and confusion and took in the talus slopes at the further end of town. Here were dotted tents, tarps and rough shacks intermingled with all the gear and simple equipment required for sluicing and panning the yellow dust.

Even from here, Will and Mike Lannigan could see the diminutive figures at work, some squatting at the edge of mountain streams and creeks, others digging with pick and shovel into the rock and dirt of the hillsides.

At night there would be lights stippled all over the place, Will figured, giving the appearance of a gigantic army of glow-worms or stationary fire-flies.

Both riders were coming in for their share of frankly curious stares from bearded miners and smooth-faced store-keepers and clerks.

Close at hand was the Golden Dollar, the most ambitious building in town, as far as Will could see. It was a two-storied structure and occupied the space of several lots. At front there was even a veranda and beyond that a tie-rack to which were hitched a couple of sorry-looking burros and three or four horses.

Kermody jerked his head towards the saloon as both men kneed their ponies across the street, dismounting and half-hitching their reins to the rack out front.

CHAPTER 3

CLEAR FORK

When Kermody shouldered his way through the batwing doors, he was struck first by the stink of last night's foul atmosphere, as yet not completely blown away by Clear Fork's mountain breezes.

The place was reasonably crowded for this

comparatively early hour, and today's thick atmosphere inside stood fair to building up before the stench of Sunday night had been completely dissipated.

Both the Pilgrim Valley riders moved slowly towards the long bar at the end of the big room, taking in details of the lay-out as they proceeded.

Kermody noted the gallery above, the baize-covered card and gaming tables and the big roulette wheel. Faro, monte, roulette, poker – everything to attract the miners' gold dust magnetically from their pokes.

Even now, there was a crowd of bearded, sweaty-faced men at the roulette wheel, tensely waiting for the girl to give the wheel another spin.

They had reached the bar now and while Lannigan called for drinks Will's speculative glance moved over the woman at the table. She was of the percentage girl type at first glance. But usually these percentage girls were not allowed to act as 'housemen' in the games of chance. This one, he thought, must be especially privileged.

She was fair-complexioned, as far as he could see, underneath the rouge and mascara, and her corn-coloured hair was piled high on top of her shapely head.

She wore a black sequin dress which clung to her magnificent figure and which revealed an expanse of dazzling shoulders and arms.

Wills studied her face again, probing beneath the mask of make-up and finding an intrinsic quality of kindness there not yet completely ironed out by the rough, crude life of this settlement.

Suddenly the Stirrup ramrod experienced a rare intuitive flash. He was sure that this girl was Laura Paramour and the thought made him recollect that in his shirt pocket was a letter from Herb and one from Ward Cabot.

Paula had sent her note to Herb Wilson by the stage-driver, but Jack Taylor would not be making the return trip until Tuesday. Thus, Will had waited for Herb to write his reply and had also brought a letter from Paula's father, Ward Cabot. This way, there would be no fear of the letters falling into Ben Mackinnon's hands, and rightly or wrongly, Will was determined to see Paula before he and Mike returned to Pilgrim Valley.

Will turned back to his drink, conscious of the fact that Mike and the barman were having words.

The bartender was a big, bullying type of a man with close-set eyes and a bearded face. Will noticed, inconsequently, that his finger-nails were black and his ham-like hands filthy. But in spite of his size, he could not boast the same terrific breadth of shoulders and barrel chest of Mike Lannigan.

'I said where you from, brother?' the barman snarled. 'We figger on knowin' our customers in the Golden Dollar. For the last time–'

Lannigan's craggy face appeared to be carved out of red rock. He leaned forward placing both hands on the bar counter; hands as big as, or bigger than, those of the tender.

'Don't threaten me,' Lannigan grated, 'you ugly, stinkin' polecat! One more wrong word outa that hole you call a mouth an' I'll bust you clean in two!'

For a long moment the two men glared at each other, anger washing over their faces, eyes glittering with savage purpose.

Will said mildly: 'He would, too, Mac. And if he didn't, I'd put a hole in your guts before you could reach that scatter-gun on the shelf.' He coolly rolled a cigarette as he spoke and when he had lit it, gently prodded the man again.

'Don't worry us, Mac,' he said, exhaling smoke in thin streamers. 'Jest get another drink.'

The bartender's glance had quickly shuttled to Kermody. He saw a powerfully built man, taller than most, and who wore a gun whose handle was smooth and black from long use. 'Mac' expelled a long, soughing breath and slowly relaxed. He knew there was nothing for it but to climb down. Now the anger was drained from him, he began to doubt whether he could have tackled even the shorter of the two men. Certainly not the tall one, he decided quickly, and both together would be suicide. If only that dam' fool side-kick of Ben Mackinnon – Art Millar – had been at the bar instead of at the roulette table. Now the man was having a row with Laura, judging by the shindig going on.

Will and Mike both turned as the sound of argument grew. There was a babble of voices and one man was leaning across the table pointing a huge, accusing finger at the white-faced girl.

'You goddam twisting bitch!' he snarled, his voice high-pitched with anger. 'Thet's the second time this week you've gone an' flicked the wheel after the ball was fallin' on my number!'

He reached forward and grabbed the girl's arm with a savage jerk, causing her to half-fall across the table on her face, her legs threshing wildly in the air.

'I'll teach you to try and double-cross Art Millar, you dirty little tramp–'

His words were suddenly cut short as a huge hand caught him by the collar of his coat, spinning him round, for all his bulk, and causing him to relinquish his grip on the half-sobbing girl.

'That's no way to treat a lady,' Will said mildly and dealt him a wicked, slicing blow on the face with the flat of his other hand.

The solid impact of that hit was like a pistol-shot in the sudden silence of the bar. Will glanced towards Mike, smiling a little, as he saw the Slash M man watching the bartender.

'*Lady*!' Art Millar screamed, staggering back against the table. 'Why, you goddam' interferin' bustard! Thet girl ain't no better'n a– And as fer you, mister–'

Will stepped in, quickly and savagely thrusting his bent elbow into Art Millar's chest, causing the flow of obscenities to be stillborn.

Millar lurched back again, sending the baize-covered table crashing to the ground. Blood was on his swarthy cheek from where Will's flat hand had struck and blood now was in his eye.

His right hand dropped to the gun in its holster, but Kermody's left arm shot out, gripping Millar's shirt and vest and dragging the man towards him as though he were a child.

Will's right fist came up then with the force of a pile-driver and connected sickeningly with Art Millar's jaw. At the same time, Will's left hand released its grip and

Millar went flying across the room to crash against the upright piano in a crumpled heap. The onlookers sat still. Perhaps because they didn't mind Art Millar being beaten up; perhaps because the other man by the bar was casually holding a six-gun in his big right fist.

Kermody blew on his knuckles and reached the girl in a couple of strides. Tears had played havoc with her make-up and the eyelash black was running grotesquely. Almost, Will could have smiled if it had not been for the hurt look in the girl's eyes.

'You all right – Laura? It is Laura Paramour, isn't it?'

The blue eyes were wide now, and the red mouth opened as she gulped down her surprise.

'Why, yeah, sure, mister. I don't know who you are, but thanks a lot. Only you shouldn't have done that. Art Millar ain't a man to forget a beatin' like that. You'd best watch out, stranger. He'll be gunnin' fer you.'

Will nodded and smiled gently and Laura Paramour wondered at the change in his face when he looked that way. The harsh lines were gone and the eyes no longer seemed like blue-grey stones.

'Is there anywhere we can talk, Laura?' Will said softly.

The men were now beginning to get the table back to rights. A few were critically examining the roulette wheel, and Mike, his gun still drawn, had allowed the bartender to take a jug of water over to the recumbent Art Millar and slosh the contents in his face.

'I guess I cain't now, mister,' the girl said. 'I'm workin' until this afternoon. I'll be off at three though–'

Will nodded. 'Okay, Laura. You live here?'

She nodded her head. 'I've got a room upstairs, but we can talk in Ben's office this afternoon, if you want. That's Ben Mackinnon, but he won't be in till this evenin', if then. Say,' Laura said fixing Will with big, blue eyes, 'who are you?'

'Will Kermody, foreman of the Stirrup spread in Pilgrim Valley. This,' Will explained, pointing to Lannigan, 'is a very good friend of mine. Mike Lannigan of Slash M.'

'Howdy, Will. Howdy, Mike,' Laura said with a half-smile curving her red lips. 'Say, I've sure heard of you, Will. Paula's talked about you–'

Will cut in swiftly. 'You can tell me all that later, Laura. Meanwhile, we're going to take a look-see around town. We'll be back at three.'

Will nodded briefly to the girl and walked back to the bar to finish his drink.

The barman stood with his arms on the counter, shoulders hunched, glowering at the room in general. At back of the tables two men had got Art Millar on to chair and were giving him whisky from a shot glass.

'How much do you like Art Millar?' Kermody asked the barman suddenly.

The question was so utterly surprising, that for a moment all traces of anger and resentment were wiped clean from the ugly, bearded features.

'Not much, mister,' he grunted at last. 'But then I don't like you, either. The both of you throw your weight about a sight too much fer me. Still,' the bartender's face split slightly into what Will took to be a grin, 'I ain't sorry he took a beatin'. I gotta hand it to you, stranger, for knowin' how to manage a bar-room fight!'

'What's your name, Mac?' There was something about Will Kermody's easy manner that even the barman could not entirely resist. But he still glowered back. 'Ray Clarke. What's your'n?'

'Will Kermody. This is Mike Lannigan. Shake, Ray!'

Slowly, reluctantly, Ray's massive paw came forward and shook each man's hand in turn.

'So this is Ben Mackinnon's place, Ray?' Will said, finishing the last of his drink.

Clarke nodded. 'Good job he ain't around this mawnin'. He wouldn't 'a' liked seein' Art beaten up. He might 'a'–' Ray closed his mouth firmly, deciding to say no more.

'You keep an eye on Laura, Ray, will you?' Kermody said, turning to go.

'Why?' Clarke demanded sourly.

Will stopped. 'I rather like you, Ray,' he said mildly. 'I'd hate to kill you...'

Ray Clarke shivered slightly as his eyes met Will Kermody's bleak gaze, but in a moment the Stirrup rider was smiling gently as he reached into his Levis and came out with a twenty-dollar gold piece.

He planked it onto the counter and Ray's hairy hand covered it in a flash.

'That should cover the drinks, Ray,' Will said. 'Be seeing you!'

They stood on the board-walk outside the Golden Dollar, idly surveying the street, waiting in case Art Millar should feel inclined to continue the fight outside.

Will's head moved slowly from side to side. 'I figure Art Millar will make his play when he's been dealt a better hand.'

Mike nodded sombrely. 'We'll haveta watch our backs, Will, 'specially after dark. What now?'

'Like a darned fool, I didn't ask Clarke where Ben's ranch was–'

'I did,' Lannigan smiled, 'after you'd knocked Millar across the room. Ben's got a small spread a coupla miles south. Clarke said there was a narrow trail startin' from the end of Main.'

'Good,' Kermody said as both men unhitched their mounts and began to walk them down-street. 'Reckon we might eat soon, Mike.'

They walked on slowly, boots churning the still soggy ground and Kermody's gaze moved over everything within range.

He saw more prospectors' shacks, mere tar-paper hovels, some of them with unglazed windows across which burlap flapped in the stirring breeze.

There were more saloons and more crude buildings and tents whose owners barked their wares to the passers-by. Will saw everywhere the basic essentials for life and death. Food, liquor, hardware and guns, apart from general stores and mining equipment.

A man emerged suddenly from a clapboard building on the other side of the street. He crossed over to the two cattlemen and stood spraddle-legged in front of them.

Will saw a tall, stringy man, tough enough for all this beanpole length, and surly-looking into the bargain.

He wore a weather-stained stetson on the back of his head, a dirty woollen shirt over which was an ancient calf-skin vest, greasy whipcord trousers and worn-down cow-boots. On the vest was a marshal's gleaming star.

His face, Kermody saw, was the colour of an old saddle and looked about as tough.

Bisecting the dark-skinned bony features were a pair of dark long-horn moustaches streaked with grey hairs and nicotine stains.

He stood, thumbs in belt, his right hand bare inches from a long-barrelled holstered Walker Colt.

'Heerd you had some trouble back at the Golden Dollar, stranger,' he said in a surprisingly thin, flat voice.

'News travels fast around here,' Will said mildly.

The marshal moved his head a few degrees and spat a thin stream of tobacco juice, just close enough to Kermody's boots to make the action offensively calculated.

'Strangers report in to me fust, if they wanta stay in Clear Fork,' he murmured. 'Who are you?'

Kermody considered the question, deciding immediately that the marshal, in spite of his crude manners and offensive ways, had a right to know.

'I'm Will Kermody, foreman of Stirrup, Pilgrim Valley—'

'I'm Mike Lannigan, owner of the Slash M from the same district,' Mike drawled. 'Since we's exchangin' cairds, what's the name of Clear Fork's marshal?'

'Charlie Ridewell's the name,' the marshal grunted. 'And if I was you two buckoos, I'd sure steer clear of Art Millar and Ben Mackinnon. I'll give you this advice for free,

Kermody. We don't go fer trouble-makers here, an' if you an' your side-kick's around by sun-down, I'll wanta know why.'

'What happens if we are, Marshal?' Will asked interestedly.

'Finish your business, whatever it is, an' git outa Clear Fork,' Ridewell said, and now his voice held the quality of steel. 'We jest natcherally don't take a shine to strangers!'

Kermody looped his mount's reins over his left arm while his hard gaze beat on to the marshal's face. The blue-grey eyes held Ridewell's bright black ones until the latter's gaze shifted slightly and dropped.

Will's voice was little more than a whisper. 'We don't like being crowded, Marshal, even if it is by the law, and we don't like threats. Art Millar's got a busted jaw and he's dam' lucky there's no lead in his belly. As for Ben Mackinnon, why, Marshal, he's an old friend of ours. Reckon you've got Mike and me all wrong. So long,' Will smiled. 'Be seeing you!'

The Stirrup foreman pushed forward as though the marshal were just not there and Ridewell was forced to give ground. The two men heard the low-muttered string of obscenities and grinned. Kermody had pierced the outer shell of the tough marshal of Clear Fork.

'There's a Chink restaurant, Will,' Mike said presently. 'Let's get outa the sun an' eat!'

Kermody nodded his agreement and the men found enough shade for both horses at the rack. The sun was hot now and the time was nearing noon.

They found a vacant booth in the crowded restaurant and both men listened to the high buzz of talk around them while they waited for their dinner.

Old Lije Merridew had found some pay-dirt this morning in Blue-fly Creek, one man said. Another confidently predicted that the rock he was busting was solid gold way underneath. How far underneath he wasn't quite sure, and guffaws of laughter greeted this naïve admission.

Purposely, Will and Mike had ordered steaks, knowing full well the difficulties of procuring beef in a mining camp where men lived from hand to mouth and largely on credit until they struck pay-dirt at least.

Both, therefore, were mildly surprised when the Chink waiter brought them rare steaks of gargantuan proportions, garnished with fried onions and fried potatoes.

'It smells good, Will,' Lannigan said as he began to tackle the heaped-up plate in front of him.

'It ought to be, Mike, if it's Stirrup or Slash M beef.' The thought was a sobering one and the Pilgrim Valley men applied themselves to their meal in silence.

Once or twice Will caught snatches of

conversation from adjoining booths and tables wherein the word 'beef' was used, but the general noise of talk was so loud and the clatter of dishes and men's shifting boots was such as to preclude the possibility of hearing any sort of detailed conversation.

They finished off with a large wedge of apple-pie and syrupy, black coffee. The food was not only plentiful, but good. At least Clear Fork did itself proud as regards food and drink, Will thought.

Kermody was in no hurry to move, as the seed of an idea fell and slowly germinated in his mind.

Soon now the restaurant started emptying. Some of the miners were anxious to get back to their diggings. Some, no doubt, wanted hard liquor, for which they had the choice of five or six saloons. Others, probably, would crawl away to sleep, and at the further end of town Will had noticed a collection of buildings that reminded him of many such 'red-light' districts he had seen...

The restaurant was empty except for Mike and Will. The waiter began clearing the tables and Will moved casually towards the kitchen, from whose doorway the yellow face of Chen Luing appeared at intervals.

Kermody leaned against the door and smiled gently. 'Dam' good steaks, Chen Luing.'

The Chinaman beamed and bobbed his

head as the quick-moving hands deftly set the kitchen to rights.

'You like Chen Luing's cooking mister?' he grinned.

'Sure,' Will said. 'I'd sure like to know where you get such tender beef.'

'Mister M'kinnon,' Chen Luing replied. 'He has ranch couple of miles south. He big man around Clear Fork. Sure. He bring Chen Luing good beef at good price!'

'I see,' Will said gently. 'Any particular brand?'

The Chink's almond eyes went dead. Will could almost see the brain working behind that opaque, slant-eyed gaze.

'Mister M'kinnon's brand. Sure. His own beef. Bar 52!'

CHAPTER 4

BEN MACKINNON

At a little after three o'clock, Will re-entered the Golden Dollar, narrowing his eyes to the smoky gloom, after the bright sunlight outside.

Ray Clarke saw the Stirrup man and jerked his head as Will Kermody crossed to the bar. There was a shot glass ready and waiting, full of rye, and the bartender pointed a stubby finger at it. Will noted that sometime between now and his first visit Clarke had somehow found time to wash his hands, though the nails were still rimmed with dirt.

'Laura's at back in the boss's office, Kermody,' Ray said. 'Figgered you might want a drink fust!'

Will nodded and grinned. He seemed to have figured out Ray Clarke fairly accurately. The man's nature was paradoxical, being a mixture of rough, almost sour good-naturedness with a leavening of bullying meanness. He had probably had to use the more unpleasant side of his disposition in this tough settlement so frequently that when his mood changed it was an agreeable surprise to himself as well as to onlookers!

Kermody downed the drink and followed the direction of Clarke's pointing finger. At the end of the bar were two doors; the nearest, Clarke explained, led directly into Mackinnon's office.

Will opened the door and came through, closing it gently behind him.

Shock at what he saw rippled through his body and rocked him back on his boot-heels.

Seated at Ben's massive roll-topped desk was a girl. Not Laura Paramour as he had expected but *Paula Mackinnon*!

58

'Hallo, Will,' she said in a carefully controlled voice. 'It's sure good to see you after all this time. Take a seat and tell me what brings you here.'

Will still stood transfixed, unable to move, gazing down at the woman who was only faintly recognizable as the Paula Cabot he had known at Stirrup.

Her heavily mascara'd eyes lifted to his face and there was the ghost of a smile on her painted lips.

'I guess I must look different from when you saw me last, Will. Maybe you don't know, but I wrote to Herb Wilson—'

Will nodded and said soberly: 'Herb showed me the letter, Paula. I've got his reply with me and a letter from Ward.'

She smiled. 'If you've read my letter to Herb, you'll understand now what I meant by helping Ben and working by his side...'

Sudden light flashed through Kermody's jolted brain. 'You mean Ben's bought this place and you and Laura Paramour work as "housemen", as percentage girls?'

Paula nodded. 'Are you so very shocked and disgusted, Will? I really have very little option!' There was the faintest trace of bitterness in Paula's voice.

Kermody drew a chair towards him, straddled it with his long legs and at last removed his hat. He laced his hands together along the upright back of the chair.

'Shocked?' Will said slowly. 'Not *at* you, Paula, only *for* you.' He gazed at her in silence for a moment, taking in the raven beauty of her dark hair; her grey eyes; the soft loveliness of her creamy shoulders and arms, which were enticingly revealed by the low-cut gown.

There was a wanton and artificial beauty here, Will realized suddenly, out of key with the *natural* beauty that he had known and remembered from when Paula used to ride the range and help with the chuck-wagon at round-up times.

'This is all Ben's doing?' Kermody's voice was deadly flat. He commenced rolling a cigarette and sent his enquiring gaze across to the girl.

That rather wistful smile came again and lights gleamed in the black hair as she nodded.

'Yes to both questions, Will. You may smoke, and it is Ben's doing, as you call it...'

Her face moved away from the shadow as she spoke and for the first time Will saw clearly the swollen and darkly shaded eye, hardly noticeable at first by virtue of the heavy make-up.

'Did he hit you, Paula? Goddam' it, I can see for myself. Why do you stay? There's a place waiting for you at Stirrup. Ward's been fretting ever since you went. I think he's only had one-two letters from you!'

'I'm sorry about Dad,' she said softly, blinking back the tears that sparkled brightly in her eyes. 'I cain't leave Ben, Will. He needs me and I'm married to him. We've all got to pay for our mis–'

'Mistakes?' Will snarled. 'Who says a woman's got to stay with her husband when he ill-treats her? Cuts her off from her friends?'

'No one says it, maybe, Will. But they think it and so does the woman herself.'

'I'm going to have to talk with Ben, by God–'

Alarm flared in Paula's eyes as she rose suddenly from the chair at the desk.

'Will, don't!'

He caught the alarm and panic in her voice, in her whole body.

'Don't you see, Will, it would be the worst sort of thing you could do to me! Once Ben knows that I've talked to you – "betrayed him", he will call it – he'll make my life a hell on earth–'

'Then you can leave him, Paula,' Kermody gritted savagely, swinging away from the chair and catching the girl in his arms.

The heady perfume made his senses swim. The feel of her warm arms in the grip of his roughened hands goaded him on so that against her will he pulled her close, pressing his mouth hard on the soft, tremulous lips.

61

For a second, perhaps, she responded, until fear, and disgust with herself, strengthened the core of her resistance.

She pushed away, half sobbing, naked misery showing for a moment in her wide eyes.

'That won't solve anything, Will,' she said, her breasts rising and falling underneath the tight corsage of her dress. 'It will only make things worse. Much worse!'

The Stirrup foreman nodded soberly and rolled another cigarette. They both needed a breathing space in which to recover.

Paula went back to her chair and repaired the ravages to her make-up with cosmetics and a mirror taken from her reticule.

'Ray and Laura told me that there were two men from Pilgrim Valley, Will.'

Kermody said: 'Mike Lannigan. You remember Slash M?'

'I remember Mike,' Paula said, 'and Phil and Dad and the Schmidts and Herb and you and all my friends—'

'Mike's nosing around town now, Paula,' Will went on. 'We're on the trail of stolen beef. Whether you like it or not, we've got to brace Ben about it.'

'You think Ben's been rustling Pilgrim Valley beef?'

'Someone's brought Stirrup and Slash M stuff as far as Clear Fork. Not many, it's true, but if we don't do something about it it'll grow, and Slash M can't afford to lose a single steer!'

'What are you going to do, Will?'

'I haven't any plan except to go out to Ben's ranch and tackle him with these...' Will took the two strips of hide from his pocket and showed Paula the brands.

'He won't admit it, Will, even if he had a hand in it!'

'I don't expect him to, Paula, but it might make him get jumpy. It might make him do something quickly that will point the finger.'

'I can't tell you anything about it, Will,' the girl said in a flat voice.

'Do you think I'd ask you?' he said softly. 'I don't even have to ask you where Ben's place is–'

Surprisingly, then, the black-haired girl turned from the desk and came over to Kermody, laying her shapely hands lightly on his arms.

'Ben will be at the ranch until ten o'clock tonight. Then he'll ride into town. Will, please be careful – for my sake!'

'This won't be the showdown with Ben, Paula,' Will told her confidently. 'This is only in the nature of a scout. Ben won't admit anything, but I'm curious to see the Bar 52.'

'Be careful, Will,' Paula pleaded again, 'and watch out for the marshal! Charlie Ridewell's a tough hombre and he's in

Ben's pocket.'

Kermody reached into his shirt pocket and withdrew the two letters.

'I almost forgot,' he grinned apologetically.

Almost avidly Paula seized them, immediately thrusting them into the bosom of her dress.

'Thanks, Will,' she breathed. 'I shall love reading them when I'm alone.' She pointed to a door in the wall opposite. 'You can go that way, Will. It leads to the rear of the building.'

Kermody smiled and put out his hand and Paula returned his grip.

'Be seeing you, Paula. Keep your chin up!'

She whispered 'Good luck' and in a moment he was gone. She sat by the desk, fighting back the tears that slowly welled her eyes…

Will Kermody rode his roan-and-white Stirrup pony down the last stretch of Main. On the right was the 'red-light' district which he had noted earlier in the day. On his left, the buildings continued along to form the three sides of a square, making a convenient site for law or protest meetings. Especially the former, Will thought grimly as his narrowed gaze took in the giant cottonwood whose cast shadow, lengthened by the lowering sun, was half-way across this open piece of ground.

Mike Lannigan sat in a disused and broken-down buggy drawn up near a tie-rack on the side of the street. He raised his arm as Kermody came towards him.

The two men glanced idly round, as though by tacit consent determining thereby the extent of their privacy. 'You see Laura?' Mike asked, satisfied that no one else was within earshot.

'I saw *Paula*,' Will said evenly. 'Rigged out like Laura, only more so!'

Lannigan's thick brows rose. 'What's she doin', Will? Working as a percentage girl?'

Kermody nodded. 'Ben's bought the place and he's making his own wife work along with Laura Paramour.'

Lannigan climbed down from the buggy and casually untied his mount from the nearby rack.

He swung into leather, nimbly for such a blocky man, and reined in alongside Kermody's gelding.

Will pointed to where the south trail swung out of town, a narrow road at first, running between the buildings which formed Clear Fork's town square.

They spurred their mounts gently and trotted through the alley-way ahead and out on to the open trail. Dust lifted lazily from the newly dried ground, stirred up by the hoofs of their ponies.

Lannigan glanced at the sun dipping behind the Goya range.

'Oughta make it by dusk, Will.'

He paused a moment before continuing, sensing that Kermody's mind was still more than half absorbed with thoughts of Paula Mackinnon.

'Heard one-two things in town, Will,' he said at last, 'even though I did have to sample some of the worst red-eye ever.

'Coupla hombres talkin' in the Bonanza Saloon. That was the last place I visited. Figgered I wasn't goin' to learn anythin' till these two mavericks started loosenin' up.'

'Let's have it, Mike,' Kermody murmured.

'They mentioned a gent by the name of Selby Lynn, Will, and I heard talk of beef bein' moved. Ben's name came into it, too, but one of the men swore and told the other to quit usin' names as well known as that.

'I couldn't overhear everything, but there was some talk of hides and blottin' and once I thought I heard Pilgrim Valley mentioned.'

Will nodded. 'We haven't anything concrete to go on, and certainly no proof to offer the law, but *we* know there's fire under the smoke and it starts right here in Clear Fork.'

'Sure,' Mike said. 'Either Clear Fork or Ben Mackinnon's ranch. Same thing, I guess.'

Will's gaze was ahead on the cluster of buildings some quarter-mile or so from the ragged trail.

He slowed the gelding to a walk and studied the ranch-house and out-buildings for sign of life. In the distance was a scattering of cattle and near to a tree-fringed stream four or five horses were picketed.

'Ben Mackinnon's Bar 52,' Will said, and swung his horse off the trail and on to the bunch-grass that stretched to within fifty or sixty yards of the house.

Both riders had passed through the gate in the fenced yard when a slight figure emerged from the gathering shadows of the house.

'*Hold et!*' the man commanded in a soft voice which yet carried clearly to the Pilgrim Valley riders.

Will pulled on the reins, bringing the gelding to a halt. Mike was slightly behind and a little to one side.

'We're looking for Ben Mackinnon,' Will said mildly, and was careful to keep both hands on the saddle-horn.

'What makes you figger he's here?' the man asked with unnecessary belligerence.

Kermody studied him for a moment, recognizing the breed immediately. He was a rubber-stamped 'gunman', from the thin hatchet face to the claw-like hands hovering over the butts of the two guns tied low down on his thighs.

A wicked impulse rode Will Kermody

then, so that his body tensed imperceptibly in the saddle as he used his knees to bring the Stirrup pony round a little. To anyone watching, it looked as though the horse was a mite restless. Now Kermody's right side was to the little gunman.

'We figured maybe Ben could answer a few questions about some stolen beef,' Will goaded.

'Sure,' Mike put in, catching on to Kermody's tactics. 'Kinda figgered he might know about butchered cows from Pilgrim Valley and buried hides.'

Lannigan, unwisely, had kneed his horse forward to make this speech, and Will knew a moment's crowding fear before the realization swept over him that Mike had gone too far.

He saw the shadowy figure crouch and move with the suddenness of forked lightning. A gun flashed in the twilight and flame lanced from the barrel as the Colt's bark merged with the swift scream of a bullet. Will even heard the soft thud as the slug lodged somewhere in Mike's body. But, long before that, Kermody's own gun had appeared as though by magic and before the gunman could draw another bead Will's Colt barked out and the little man's gun was sent flying from his numbed hand as Will's bullet smashed into the cylinder.

Even then the Bar 52 killer would have

gone for his other gun, but Kermody put a bullet into the ground a few inches from the man's left boot. He stood like a carved statue and Will said, *'Don't try it!'*

A light sprang up in the house and a door opened. They heard Ben's bull-like voice as it roared out into the oncoming night.

'What's going on out there, Nick? *Goddammit, answer me, will you?'*

Nick slowly relaxed but his bright gaze never left Will's face. 'Coupla saddle-bums makin' big talk, Ben,' he gritted. 'Better watch the tall bustard–'

Mackinnon came forward slowly, a long gun cocked and ready in his hand. Will shot a quick glance at Mike, who was holding his damaged shoulder and swaying slightly in the saddle. The ramrod kept his voice level. 'It's Will Kermody and Mike Lannigan. Mike's been hit. Put up the gun and call off your watch-dog, Ben!'

Ben Mackinnon's boisterous laugh bellowed out as he took in the situation and spoke to his gunman as though he were indeed a dog.

'Get back to the bunk-house, Flore,' Ben snarled, 'and stay there.'

His voice was weighted with such contempt that Will looked for the expected reaction of resentment. Surprisingly, however, Nick Flore nodded his head, bent down to retrieve his damaged gun and slunk off into the darkness of the out-buildings like a whipped cur.

Ben was all bluff heartiness now as he apologized for the reception they had been given. His huge bulk moved quickly into the house as he lit oil lamps and indicated for Will to place Lannigan on the large sofa near the open fire.

Like everything about Mackinnon, the ranch-house was quite vast, deceptively so from the outside, Will thought.

The living-room in which they were now seated ran from front to back of the house on one side. At the near end were wide french windows, part covered now by heavy brocade curtains of fine quality.

Against the chilly coolness of the on-coming night a log fire blazed merrily in the hearth. There were deep leather chairs scattered around the huge room (comfort almost unheard of even in a wealthy rancher's place) and Kermody's swift-moving gaze took in the array of liquor bottles on the heavy, ornately carved dresser; the shining silverware and the profusion of attractive coal-oil lamps.

Mackinnon, standing with his back to the fire, had shouted some unintelligible order through the open door and now an impassive-faced oriental came hurrying in, laden with a bowl of water and surgical dressings.

'Su Y'han will make Mike comfortable,' Ben reassured the Stirrup ramrod. 'He knows a thing or two about gun-shot cases. Lannigan'll be fit as a fiddle after a sleep. I reckon you'd both better stay here overnight, Will, now that you've visited up with me after all this time!'

Kermody found difficulty in hugging bitterness and hatred to his bosom in the face of Ben's almost overwhelming hospitality and apparent pleasure at seeing them.

He studied the big man frankly, while Ben himself crossed to the dresser and sloshed whisky into tall glasses as though it were water.

He had on a fine, broadcloth cut-away coat that had been moulded to those powerful rolling shoulders by an artist. The trousers matched the coat and were tucked into hand-tooled, high-heeled boots, *sans* spurs.

Across Ben's colossal torso was a fancy waistcoat, bisected by a heavy gold chain. His face was heavier than Will remembered, more roan-flushed and florid, but the big eyes were bold underneath the busy brows and quick moving as of old.

His hair was still as thick, though slicked down with pomade, and the ends of his black moustaches were very evidently waxed.

Here was a man, Will considered, of vast

physique and tremendous purpose. A man who could never pass unnoticed in a crowd. A man who exuded bluff *bonhomie* as well as a dynamic driving force. Business acumen, even utter ruthlessness, yet seemingly tempered with cordiality and tolerance for the weaker ones. That was the picture Ben Mackinnon presented to the world; yet, Will thought, *the man's living a lie!*

Kermody took the proffered glass and drank gratefully. He felt he needed this. Evidently Ben felt the same way, for he poured half the whisky down his throat without pause and without batting an eyelid. Will figured he must have drunk best part of a half-pint at a single gulp.

Ben slammed down his glass on the broad shelf over the fireplace and grinned, showing even white teeth.

He nodded to where Mike lay; where the Chinaman was finishing the dressing.

'Mike'll be all right, Will. You see. That Chink bustard sure knows a helluva lot for a heathen.'

Again Will felt surprise at the absence of any resentment in the eyes of the person thus referred to. Instead, Su Y'han looked up and grinned as though pleased at some compliment. He looked enquiringly at Will's glass, then shuttled his gaze to the man on the couch.

Kermody came forward, putting the glass

72

to Mike's lips and forcing him to drink some of the spirit.

Lannigan's eyes fluttered open and he breathed a feeble 'Thanks.'

'You sleep now, Mike,' Will said. 'You'll feel better when you wake up.'

The Chink had disappeared and Lannigan was breathing evenly, stretched full-length on the sofa.

Ben grinned widely. 'Well, Will. What brings you to Bar 52 and Clear Fork? I take it you came through our town?'

Will said softly, 'Looking for sign of stolen beef, Ben,' and withdrew the branded hide cuttings from his pocket. For a second, naked anger sparked and flared in Mackinnon's eyes. Will was sure it was anger and not fear. But it was gone in a flash, so quickly that the ramrod wondered whether it had merely been the reflection of his own imagination.

Mackinnon laughed now. 'What have these to do with me, Will? You're not suggesting that I *rustle* beef, are you?' He laughed again, boisterously, and clapped Will on the back with a force that would have shaken an average man.

'You always were a bit of a curious hombre, Will, Bit too serious-minded, I'd say. But never mind that. You and Lannigan are my guests for as long as you care to stay.

'I've got to go to town tonight, but the

73

house is yours, Will, and Su Y'han will give you anything you want–'

'I'd like to come with you, Ben,' Will said mildly.

'Well, now, Will. There ain't no need for that at all. You've ridden all the way from Pilgrim Valley. I guess you could use a rest now. You jest stay right here.'

'I'm coming into town, Ben,' Will said flatly, and for a long moment two strong personalities clashed and fought a silent battle as two pairs of eyes locked with each other.

Ben's gaze dropped first and again he was the bluff, genial host.

'Sure, Will. If that's what you want, we'll ride in together. I'll show you my place 'less'n you've already sampled the Golden Dollar?'

Will smiled thinly. 'The Golden Dollar and I are old friends, Ben.'

CHAPTER 5

'SADDLE THE GRULLA, TIM!'

Round-up was continuing apace and Phil Hankins was religiously carrying out the last-minute instructions that Will had given before lighting out for Clear Fork.

Jim Stewart and Fay Murphy were still over to the eastern section of Stirrup range, but here, in the breaks of the Cedar Creek, on this western boundary, Phil Hankins, Sid Vincent, Dave Swallow and Brecker Chase were hard at work with Fred Robards of Lannigan's Slash M.

Ward Cabot himself was there, doing his hard share of work like any waddy and wondering from time to time what Will was doing and how Paula was faring.

Young Tim Furnival was with the chuck-wagon and preparing the meals as well as keeping an eye on the *remuda*. Chuck Anderson, the Stirrup cook, had stayed behind at the ranch to keep a general watch on things.

In the heat of the afternoon, they sweated on, ear-marking, burning brands, cutting out Slash M from Stirrup beef and throwing a few Circle D steers across Pilgrim River back on to Ed Narroway's range.

Sam Bassett of Circle D was 'rep' for Ed Narroway and mavericks, combed from the river breaks of the Pilgrim or chased from the northern foothills, were equally divided between the three spreads irrespective.

Tim Furnival had a mess fire going near the chuck-wagon, and towards this Ward Cabot and Phil Hankins rode. Both were tired, sweaty and dust-caked and wiped their streaming faces with limp bandanas.

'Pour us a cup of coffee, Tim,' Cabot called to the young wrangler, 'then cut me out that grulla–'

'Ain't you done enough for today, boss?' Phil Hankins asked, his young, lean face showing concern.

Cabot grinned in spite of being pre-occupied with his thoughts.

'We've got another couple of hours good, yet, Phil,' he objected, 'and I ain't aimin' to waste the time. 'Specially with Will away.'

'We kin use all the help we kin get,' Hankins drawled. 'You know that, but I wouldn't figger on ridin' that grulla!'

Both men had dismounted, trailing their reins, and Tim Furnival quickly unsaddled and unbridled the sweating beasts, turning them into the brush and pole corral.

He dumped the gear on the ground and came back to pour coffee for Ward and the *segundo*.

'Phil's right, Mr. Cabot,' Tim said with earnest concern. 'Thet grulla ain't properly gentled yet. As mean a side-winder as ever busted a cinch and threw its rider!'

Cabot laughed, but a spasm almost of temper crossed his face, sharpening the easy-going features. 'You figger I cain't ride anythin' you got in that *remuda*, Tim?' he snapped. 'Why, son, I was gentling tougher broncs than that afore you was dry behind the ears!'

Tim flushed and bit back the sharp reply that rushed to his lips. Silently he handed Phil and Ward their cups of steaming coffee.

From the branding fire a few hundred yards away came the squeal of hog-tied beasts as the irons burned into their tough, hairy hides.

The sharp smell of scorching skin and hair was a familiar and not unpleasant odour to these cowboys and in no way interfered with their enjoyment of chuck-wagon food and freshly boiled coffee.

'Tim's right, boss,' Phil Hankins said, flinging the dregs from his cup on to the dry ground and hitching up his belt. 'They's other fresh mounts there besides the grulla, Ward.'

Cabot said: 'Maybe. But you oughta know by now, Phil, that when my mind's made up I can be right smart ornery myself.' And then, as though to end a discussion with which he had grown bored, he added, 'Saddle the grulla, Tim!'

Young Furnival's glance lifted to the *segundo's* face, but Phil merely shrugged, realizing the futility of argument once an easy-going man like Ward Cabot had dug his heels in.

Tim had kept the grulla on a long picket rope and even now he threw the blanket and saddle across its back only with the greatest difficulty. The pony arched and then blew out its belly and bared its teeth, jabbing at Tim whenever possible with its writhing mouth.

Phil and Ward watched the proceedings, the *segundo* with a feeling of mounting alarm, and Cabot apparently with a casual admiration for the young wrangler's handling of the intractable beast.

Tim felt the horse's big teeth snap at his hands as he bridled the head and inserted the bit. Finally he struck the distended belly a sharp blow, forcing the grulla to slacken its taut muscles and expel the held-in air. Only then was he able to adjust the cinch straps correctly.

He held the beast almost cruelly on the shortened picket rope until Ward was in leather. Then the wrangler slipped the knot and the horse was free to unseat the rider atop.

Ward Cabot had been a top hand in his time and still retained enough of his cunning to handle most ornery critturs. But the grulla was rotten-meat right through to its heart and Tim had only brought it along in the vague hopes of trying to gentle it further.

At the branding fire the Stirrup men looked across to where Tim Furnival's chuck-wagon stood close to the makeshift corral. Brecker Chase narrowed his gaze and swore softly.

'That's the boss atop thet killer hoss, Birdie,' he said to Dave Swallow. 'Whyfer does Ward hev to do such a goddam' crazy thing–?'

Sid Vincent said: 'The grulla's startin' its tricks now. Even the boss won't stay long in that saddle!'

Ward sensed his mistake as soon as the grulla was free from the restraining picket rope. He knew it had been a prideful sort of obstinacy which had caused him to ignore the warnings of Phil and Tim and he knew now, without any doubt, that there were few men, apart perhaps from Will Kermody, who could stay in the grulla's saddle over a few seconds.

Now Cabot hauled on the reins as the horse began bucking and sun-fishing; leaping into the air and coming down on all four legs with bone-shattering force. It arched and reared, twisted and turned and with a sudden wicked urge tried to smash its rider against the flimsy pole-fence.

Even Ward's considerable strength seemed to avail little against that cruel, iron mouth. Again the Stirrup owner was bounced clear of the saddle by another sudden bucking side-jump and again Ward managed to maintain his seat and keep booted feet in the stirrups.

Hot-tied steers were forgotten for the moment as Stirrup's men together with

79

Fred Robards and Sam Bassett watched with anxious yet excited expressions.

Phil Hankins had uncoiled the rope from his saddle, set now on roping the grulla before Ward should be pitched, perhaps to his death. It was time to ignore the obstinacy of a man, the *segundo* figured, as he carefully built his loop.

For some reason Ward had wanted to show the men that he was just as good as his hands, perhaps better, and now the time for such foolishness was long gone.

Hankins, preparing for his throw, saw what he had dreaded from the first.

The grulla, with blood-filled nostrils, and unable to shake free the man on its back, suddenly reared up on hind legs until it was almost vertical.

Cabot, clinging desperately to reins and stirrups, fought grimly to get the beast's head down, but so far back had the grulla reared that Ward's bloodshot eyes were now gazing skywards. With a surge of quickening fear, he felt the animal begin its backward fall. In a few seconds or less it would have turned turtle and would be crashing down on the rider.

Ward's booted feet began to slide from the stirrup's, but even as the grulla crashed over backwards, Ward Cabot found his left foot caught in the near-side stirrup of the stock saddle.

The horse crashed over on its back, rolling on to its side and pinning Ward's left leg underneath its heavy body.

At the last moment Ward had twisted violently in an effort to wrench his foot free of its encumbrance, but in so doing, and with the weight of the horse atop, he felt the pure flame of searing pain that told his blurred and jarred senses that his leg was broken.

Two or three of the men who had broken away from the branding-fire group tugged at the thrashing grulla while Phil Hankins hacked through the stirrup-leather on the near side, eventually freeing Ward's grotesquely twisted leg.

'Get him into the chuck-wagon, boys!' Hankins commanded. 'You, Tim, saddle up a hoss an' ride into town for Doc Laurie. Fetch him to the house. We'll get Ward back to the ranch in the wagon.'

Young Furnival was already saddling his own particular mount before the *segundo* had finished giving his instructions. Sid Vincent said: 'I'll drive back in the wagon with you, Phil, and give a hand. Brec can look after things here until tomorrow.'

Hankins nodded. 'Yeah. I'll need some help with him. Thanks, Sid. You carry on here, Brec, will you?'

Chase nodded. 'We got another fifty head to brand and ear-mark before dark. You'll be out again tomorrow?'

'Sure.' Then, as a thought struck him, Hankins turned to the young wrangler already atop his saddled horse.

'See if you can get Miss Owen along as well, Tim. Thar ain't anyone else around as could nurse Ward like her.' The men exchanged glances, knowing that Hankins was thinking of the absent Paula, but Tim merely nodded, touching spurs to his pony and bending low in the saddle, heading straight for town.

A three-quarter moon was drenching the night range with its silver-golden light, when Will and Ben set out from the Bar 52 for Clear Fork.

With Mackinnon's glib and easy talk as a background, Will's thoughts had been busy during the last few hours. It was difficult to imagine such a 'big' man descending to meanness and cruelty with regard to his own beautiful wife. And yet, Will reflected, the evidence was there, plain enough for anyone to see. Particularly plain for an old friend, such as himself.

Strangers, perhaps, might notice nothing untoward between Ben Mackinnon and his wife, but apart from physical signs, such as the swollen and discoloured eye (and Will was certain sure it had been done by Ben), there were the less obvious indications, clear enough to an interested party, for all that.

Paula's very being felt tarnished, Will knew, with the whole set-up and her job in particular.

In order to attract custom and build up a big trade at the Golden Dollar, Ben expected, aye, insisted, that his wife appeared nightly, heavily made-up and in dresses revealing enough to have given most percentage girls cause for objection.

And how did Laura Paramour fit into all this?

Will considered the girl in his mind; what he knew about her; and realized that the sum total of his knowledge was small enough. But Paula looked upon her as a good friend and Will, remembering the honesty and gratitude in the girl's blue eyes, when the ramrod had saved her from Art Millar's wrath, inclined to the belief that whatever outward appearances might show, Laura Paramour was made of the right stuff.

There was more than a chance, of course, that Laura was Ben's mistress and that Ben, in his calculating and sadistic way, took delight in flaunting her before his wife. Yet the two women liked each other and were friends, that was sure. How could this be, then, if Will's suspicions were correct?

But Laura would have little choice in the matter in any case. Her choice such as it was, would be the same as Paula's. *Stay and do what you're told, or else get out!*

Will Kermody would blame no woman for staying, knowing the extent to which she would be branded and cast aside by folk generally, once she was out on her own.

There was no place for a girl or a woman outside the immediate protection of her seducer, in the wild west of the nineteenth century!

Will began to feel the slow rising of an anger which he knew would not now be dimmed by Ben's bluff cordiality. He was learning more of the man and his transparency in these last few hours than he had learned during the eighteen months when Mackinnon had divided his time between Selwyn and Stirrup.

That had been when Ben was a captain in the U.S. Cavalry and had made a grand, dashing figure in his uniform and mounted on his big, black horse.

Soon after that, Ben's period of service had terminated, and even the change into civilian clothes had not dimmed the wonder in Paula's eyes every time she saw him.

Now they were married. Irrevocably, according to Paula herself. Whatever hardships or difficulties she had to contend with were the natural result of her own mistakes. So Paula thought and believed. It was her duty to remain with the man she had married, and Kermody's mind leaped ahead to the only possible alternative. The idea which Herb Wilson had sown in his mind and the execution of which was the reason for Will's very presence here.

'Your Nick What's-his-name, Ben,' Will said breaking a long silence. 'A professional gun-thrower?'

'Well, now, Will,' Ben said with an amused tolerance. 'I wouldn't quite say that, although you must understand its not quite the same out here as it is even in Pilgrim Valley.

'Anyone who runs cattle or horses here,' Mackinnon went on, 'leaves himself wide open to rustling.

'I guess you have none, or very little, in the valley, but here, the strongest man takes what he wants and holds it. If he don't do that, he ain't the strongest man. It's as simple as that!'

'I hear you're the biggest man around these parts, Ben. That makes you the strongest. How does the boot feel?'

Ben winced slightly. 'I wish you'd get it out of your head that I'm building up a future by rustling and killing folk and walking on their heads, or some such thing, Will!

'I guess you just don't understand the difference between things here in Archer County and things in Pilgrim Valley.

'Maybe there's not much law there, either,

except Herb Wilson's milk-and-water methods in Selwyn. But there's a dam' sight less, here, Will. None in fact–'

'What about Marshal Ridewell?'

Ben peered ahead, looking for the lights of the settlement. They were nearly there now.

'Charlie Ridewell? Shucks, Will, he's only hired to deal with drunks and keep law and order more or less in town. He ain't got nothing to do with chasing wide-loopers or outlaws from the badlands.

'If I didn't have one-two hands like Nick Flore on the pay-roll – well, I'd sure be skinned of hide an' hair within a week!'

'You know a hombre name of Selby Lynn?'

Mackinnon's glance flashed to Will's face and for the first time Kermody saw the infinitesimal flicker of apprehension.

'Sure,' he replied after the briefest of pauses. 'Guess almost everyone knows everyone else around here, Will. He's some sort of cattle dealer, though I ain't done any business with him yet.'

'I suppose you could call rustlers cattle-dealers, couldn't you, Ben?' Will said mildly.

This time Mackinnon's glance was searching and hot. Then he slowly relaxed as though satisfied that Kermody's question was no more than an idle and perhaps badly worded remark.

For all that, Ben Mackinnon was beginning to revise his opinion of Stirrup's ramrod. There was a directness about some of Kermody's remarks; a pointedness that was not lost on the owner of Bar 52 and the Golden Dollar. Once or twice, too, Ben had caught a glimpse of the old familiar hardness in Kermody's face, only more so.

It would be a pity, Ben thought, if Will got so nosy that it became necessary to set Nick Flore or Lee Tyler or Slim Comal on to him...

They dismounted at the Golden Dollar, racked the horses and stepped across the threshold into the roar of voices, the blaze of yellow lights and the smoke-laden atmosphere of the crowded room.

It was all Ray Clarke could do, even with another man helping him, to keep pace with the demands for beer and rye whisky for eager, dust-clogged throats.

Kermody's glance flashed over the room, finishing up at the roulette table. Paula was there, bending over the wheel, her black hair glistening in the lights, her shapely, powdered shoulders and arms dazzling against the dark brilliance of her sequin dress.

Her gaze lifted as she moved back from the wheel, surprise showing faintly in her eyes as she noted that Ben and Will were together.

She had her moment of sudden certainty as she regarded the two figures, an intuitive thought-flash whispering to her that soon both these men would tear away the thin screen of mild pretence and reveal the savage strength and purpose underneath.

There would be a fight, Paula felt sure. How or where or when it would start in earnest, she did not know. For the first time since her marriage she was aware of a feeling of disloyalty towards Ben.

Automatically she called the numbers and pushed the chips across the table, taking bets and re-spinning the wheel.

Where was she? Disloyal thoughts! Thoughts which no woman should have concerning the man she had taken in wedlock. But the idea persisted and grew stronger, and she felt powerless to deny it.

Will was the man she loved and Will was the man she so desperately desired to win this fight!

CHAPTER 6

WALLS HAVE EARS

'The drinks are on the house, Will,' Mackinnon smiled, and to the bartender, 'set 'em up, Ray!'

Clarke nodded and gave his grimace of a smile. He was pleased with himself. Pleased that he had grudgingly accepted Will's proffered friendship earlier on. If this Kermody man was so friendly with the boss, it was as well he, Ray, had climbed down.

Ben excused himself on account of a busy night at the Golden Dollar. 'The place is yours, Will. Have what you want—'

Kermody nodded and watched Ben disappear through the door into his office. A moment later he came out and ascended the stairs to the galleried floor above.

Will saw a houseman come down to help Paula at the roulette table. Several percentage girls followed, each in bright, low-cut frocks, ready to dance and drink with the clamouring miners below.

Someone started up the piano and the noise of talk and laughter grew to the accompaniment of stamping feet and swirling dancers.

Will downed his third drink. Clarke, the bartender, considered it his special duty to see that Kermody's glass was refilled every so often and Will, with only his own sombre thoughts for company, sank whisky with monotonous regularity.

He saw Art Millar sitting at one of the poker tables and felt a faint stirring of pleasure as he noted the bandaged jaw.

He pushed away from the bar and threaded a way through the crowd towards

Millar's table, ploughing through men rather than walking round them. Will was not drunk but enough liquor would always bring out a certain wildness in him.

One or two burly miners swore and turned aggressively as Kermody pushed by. They looked again at the tall, weather-beaten figure, and had their second thoughts about starting anything.

Moreover there was such wicked purpose in this man's measured walk, that heads turned and conversation began to subside as they watched him stand, spraddle-legged, looking down at Art Millar.

Everyone had heard how Millar had gotten a damaged jaw and a badly cut head. Some said that this Pilgrim Valley rider had knocked him down with the flat of his hand and that Art had been unconscious for over an hour!

Now it looked like there might be more trouble as men's glances followed Kermody's high figure with a bright and eager expectancy.

Talk had dropped to a low buzz although the piano still tinkled and couples whirled their partners. Even so, those in the vicinity of Art Millar's table had no difficulty in hearing Will's opening words.

'Caught out anyone else cheating you, Art?'

Kermody's voice was coldly mocking and

a dull, red surge of rage ran the length and breadth of Millar's stubbled face.

The piano had stopped suddenly and the dancers stood still, metaphorically, if not in actual fact, caught on one foot.

Kermody's gaze probed Millar's face, his goading tone rowelled the surface of Art Millar's temper, splitting it open so that men could see the gathering fury of the man underneath the thin outer veneer.

'Better watch out for Art, boys,' Kermody said in that same cold, wicked voice. 'Don't go coppering his bets, else, like as not he'll up and twist your arm off – that is if any of you happen to be a woman.'

Somewhere at the back of the room a man's soft laugh started and finished with spine-chilling suddenness. The silence then was sticky. Nothing moved except the lazily drifting smoke swirling around the bright, overhead lights.

Millar's face had changed from crimson to white and men knew that it was not fear, but a deep, bitter, choking anger.

Will stood with thumbs in his gun-belt, and hot glances shuttled from his flat-planed face to the black-butted Colt a few inches from his right hand.

In a second now, Art Millar would go for his gun!

But the deathly silence was broken by a different kind of interruption, and from an unexpected quarter.

Ben Mackinnon's cool voice cut through that loud silence like a sharp blade swathing corn.

'*Hold it, everyone,*' he said, and all, except Kermody, turned and saw the long-barrelled Colt held in Mackinnon's rock-steady fist.

'Stay where you are, Art,' Ben went on coolly. 'Will! I want you a minute!'

For a brief moment Kermody felt the impulse to resist; to go for his gun and end this thing right now. No one could say he had not played square. All would bear witness to the fact that Ben's gun was already out and covering Kermody and the men at the poker table.

There was, however, a swell chance of ending up a corpse. Ben's marksmanship was unquestionably as good as or better than that of anyone else in the room. Will wondered whether it was better than his own, and then he turned slowly and smiled, and tension which had rolled upwards to fever pitch now receded swiftly in a vast drawn-out breath of relief.

Will moved away from the table, taking care not to place himself between Art Millar and Ben's gun.

Quickly the hum of conversation started up again. The pianist began a lively jig and in a few moments the room was back to its former uninhibited rowdiness.

'You trying to start something, Will?' Ben said, signalling Ray Clarke to pour fresh drinks.

'Only figuring on smoking out a few rats, Ben. Thought I'd start with Art Millar, the dirtiest rat I've so far discovered!'

Ben's glance travelled thoughtfully over Kermody's face. He knew that Will had purposely braced Millar in order to kill him. If ever there had been blood in a man's eye, Ben had seen it in Will Kermody's, back there a few moments ago.

'You know, Will, you and I have got something in common after all.

'I hadn't figured it before. Now I'm beginning to see it. We're both plumb determined to have what we want once our minds are set on it. Maybe we could start some kind of partnership?'

'What about Laura?' Will said softly, and for a moment the significance of the question failed to register with Mackinnon. When it did, Will saw the bright spark of comprehension flicker in Ben's bold eyes.

'You could have Laura, Will,' he said quickly, and now the ramrod considered that one of his suspicions at least had been proved beyond reasonable doubt.

Ben Mackinnon was offering him his mistress in the same way that he might offer him a pair of pistols or a share of his profits.

He was not, Will knew, offering a percentage girl, as such; an employee. He was offering a *personal possession*, and Will fought hard for a moment to keep the contempt out of his voice and to mask it from his eyes.

'You never can tell what might turn up, Ben,' he said presently. 'I'm going back now to your place. Mike and I will have to be off to an early start–'

Mackinnon was too shrewd a business man to press the point. 'All right, Will. Maybe you'll ride over here again in the near future. Think over the possibilities. There ain't anyone else around here *or* in Pilgrim Valley I'd let come in on the ground floor!...'

Will leaned against the clap-board wall of the Golden Dollar. The tip of his cigarette was a small isolated glow in the shadows of the porch.

He watched the stream of traffic – still heavy in spite of the late hour – with unseeing eyes, his mind going back over the preceding events.

He grinned, recollecting the pointed remarks he had made to Ben about rustling and even dragging in the name of Selby Lynn. But instead of flaring up, Mackinnon had cleverly side-stepped those issues, even to the point of suggesting some sort of partnership.

Will drew on his cigarette and let the

smoke trickle down his nostrils. He was still far from sure whether Ben was involved in any rustling or not, but Will had hardly expected to settle everything on this first trip.

He would come back to Clear Fork, for sure, and somehow or another this evil man would have to be fixed. Will did not doubt that Ben kept himself surrounded by gunmen at the Golden Dollar – there would be others like Art Millar – as well as killers like Nick Flore at the ranch. Ben had already admitted to having three 'hands' at the Bar 52!

Kermody ground out his cigarette beneath his boot, pushed away from the wall and crossed to the rack. He tightened the cinch-straps on the Stirrup pony and swung into leather, pointing the horse towards the Mackinnon Spread along the moonlit trail...

In an upstairs room at the Golden Dollar, Laura Paramour lay full length on her bed trying hard to relax against the time when she would have to take over again from Paula. That was always the worst time – from midnight until the place doused its lights around 2 or sometimes 3 a.m.

The drunks were more difficult then and the bright flame of temper, never far from the surface, flared more explosively when saturated with liquor. Besides which, it was a time when Ben often made himself unpleasant. Though he rarely appeared the worse for drink, it was always obvious to both Laura and Paula when Ben had taken more than usual. Odiously obvious!

Whenever Laura began to experience the old familiar surge of self-pity, she thought of Ben's wife and in spite of, or because of, the extraordinary situation, Laura Paramour felt intensely towards Paula, as though she were her own sister.

She leaned back on her pillows, her mind switching to the man Kermody, from Pilgrim Valley. The man who had braced the big, bullying Art Millar and had handled him as though he were an under-sized runt!

There was a man she thought, with a queer stab of jealousy inside her breast. If only Will Kermody–

Her ruminations were suddenly and sharply arrested by the murmur of voices from the adjoining room. The walls were thin matchboarding, and although the men's voices were lowered in recognition of this fact the words yet came faintly audible to Laura's ears.

'...I keep tellin' you, Brad,' a voice went on. 'Ben figgers to get the stuff, as much as we want, at the right price. There'll be no need to buy rustled beef from Walker any more and pay out all our profits for havin' it night-trailed all that distance!'

'How much a haid is the bustard askin', Sel?' the other voice came in.

'We haven't arranged everythin' yet, Brad. I'm seein' Ben later to settle the details. A figure of fifteen dollars a haid has been mentioned for prime stuff, cut out an' delivered where we want it, Brad–'

'Whose beef?'

There was a silence for a moment and Laura, on the other side of the thin partition, moved closer to the wall.

'Brand'll be mostly Stirrup from Pilgrim Valley, 'cos they got so much they'll be that much easier to rob. Maybe a few other brands as well.'

'Why in hell don't we cut the stuff out our own selves an' get the beef for nuthin?' Brad growled.

'Are you crazy, Brad? We ain't got night raiders an' gun-men like Mackinnon's got. He's the jasper as is takin' the risks. If thar's any come-back it'll be *his* men as gets it in the back, not ourn. Also he's prepared to deliver to our places – door to door service – an' cash on the nail!'

'All right, Selby, have it yore way,' the other grunted. 'When you fixin' this for?'

'I'm seein' Ben later tonight in his office along the passage. It won't be for a day or two. I'll see you here in Clear Fork, Brad, an' let you know!'

'You stayin' on in this room, right here?'

97

Laura Paramour heard no answer to this question, but divined that the man had nodded his assent.

The girl's face was pale under its make-up. She trembled a little as she realized the significance of the conversation she had just heard.

'Selby,' the man had said. That could only mean – *Selby Lynn*! Who Brad was, she was not sure. It didn't much matter. Selby Lynn was fixing to buy rustled beef from Ben and Ben's crew at the Bar 52 would do the work; no doubt steal the cattle and even blot the brands before delivering.

What was most important was that the bulk of the stolen cattle would be Stirrup, and Will Kermody was foreman of the Stirrup spread.

With a slight shock, Laura realized suddenly that Paula herself would be as interested a person as anyone. It was so easy in this life of theirs at Clear Fork to forget that Mackinnon's wife had been *Paula Cabot*. Now Ben was going to steal from his father-in-law, Ward Cabot, and those same steers, Laura realized, were even now partly Paula's property. When Ward died, undoubtedly the whole of the Stirrup spread would be passed on to his daughter.

Laura's shrewd brain was now working fast, as a new and dangerous thought struck her.

If Ward died, the ranch would be Paula's and Ben Mackinnon would have no need to rustle cattle. *He could help himself to whatever he wanted – more or less legally!*

It became, therefore, more important than ever that Will should be warned – if only she had been able to overhear the time and place when this rustling was to take place! But it had not yet been settled. Selby Lynn was going to arrange that with Ben, some time tonight!

Laura Paramour swung her shapely legs off the bed. It was an action symbolic of decision suddenly reached.

Was Will still in Clear Fork? she wondered, or had he returned yet to Pilgrim Valley?

The first thing, however, was to have a talk with Paula, if only she could get her without Mackinnon himself horning in. It was getting increasingly difficult of late to get Paula on her own. Now in Laura's blue-grey eyes there was a hard light, masking the normal sweet expression. Her full, red lips were pressed together signifying a quiet but steadfast determination. Here was a chance, slim though it might seem, of throwing off the hateful yoke of Ben Mackinnon's dragging grip and at the same time helping Paula and repaying the debt she owed Will Kermody for his timely aid in the saloon.

It was evident to both men, as they sat their horses in the greying light of approaching dawn, that Ben's Chinese servant had made a good job of dressing Mike's punctured arm.

Lannigan had slept a deep, health-restoring sleep last night from the time Su Y'han had finished his first aid until the moment, a bare half-hour ago, when Will had gently nudged him awake, setting down the hastily cooked breakfast and steaming java by the side of the huge sofa.

Will could see that in spite of Mike's pallor, he was sufficiently rested to attempt the ride back, even if it had to be done in easy stages.

Thanks to Su Y'han, there was no sign of poisoning, and Mike himself seemed completely free of any fever.

He ate hungrily, while Will rolled a smoke and drank some of the coffee. They spoke softly so as not to awaken Ben whose room was close by.

'You figure you can stay in the saddle, Mike?' Will said and the Slash M man grinned as best he could with a mouth full of food. He gulped down coffee and cleared his throat.

'It's a cinch, Will, though I don't say it doesn't hurt like hell. It sure does!'

'What with the Chink's medical skill and your natural toughness,' Will smiled, 'you'll make it all right.'

Mike nodded and slowly, experimentally, rose from the couch. Kermody retied Mike's bandana to form a sling for his arm, thus taking the weight off his shoulder muscles.

'That makes it easier,' the Slash M man grinned. 'Let's get to the hosses and you can give me the news on the way.'

By noon they were on the floor of Pilgrim Valley and Will, noting the greyness of Mike's usually ruddy face and the limp sway of his chunky body in the saddle, called a halt.

They watered the horses at a small creek which later joined Cedar Creek.

Mike sank wearily to the ground as the Stirrup ramrod first built a fire and then cut a few strips from a piece of bacon.

These he placed in the skillet and, while they cooked, he set the coffee-pot on the glowing coals.

Lannigan one-handedly rolled a cigarette and, when he had lit it, broke the long silence.

'You figger maybe we could've braced Ben, back there, and pinned somethin' on him, Will?'

Kermody slowly shook his head. It was a question he had already asked himself and he knew the answer was 'no'.

He smiled thinly for a moment and lifted his gaze from the mess fire.

'I very nearly did, Will, when Ben threw that gun on me when I was prodding Art Millar. I guess it was mostly the whisky talking, though.' Again Will shook his head as though to emphasize his point.

'I think we would have spoiled our chances and maybe got killed into the bargain. We've given Ben and Art Millar and Nick Flore something to think about without telling them quite what we know or how much. Even the unknown Selby Lynn, by this time, might be trying to figure us out, because I mentioned his name to Ben.'

'Ben slid round that one?'

Will said in his usual mild voice, 'Ben slid round everything almost, Mike, but I had a hard job keeping away from my gun when he suggested a partnership and offered to throw Laura in as bait!'

Mike nodded soberly. 'Both those girls are too dam' good for that life, Will.'

An hour later they were on the move, refreshed by the meal and the long rest. They rode in silence for a long time until late afternoon found them at Cedar Fork where the thick belt of willows flung out along the water on the Slash M side.

'You'd best rest up for a day or two, Mike,' Will said. 'I'll tell Fred Robards to come back and give you a hand, and I'll send Doc Laurie over tomorrow.'

'Thanks, Will, but let me know when

you're goin' to Clear Fork again. I've bought chips in this game!'

Kermody nodded and watched the Slash M owner move through the trees towards the house on the hill. Then he put his pony to the water and pointed towards the Stirrup buildings, lost in the blue-hazed folds of the darkening range.

CHAPTER 7

GLOWING THOUGHTS!

Phil Hankins swung down from the veranda and came to meet Kermody in the night-shadowed yard.

Tim Furnival took the ramrod's horse as Phil gave his news briefly and without embellishment.

'Is he bad hurt?' Kermody asked, moving towards the ranch-house.

'Doc Laurie figgers he'll be all right, Will. He ain't in much pain now, but it's doubtful whether he'll sit a saddle later on.'

Kermody nodded and stepped quickly into the house, making his way to Ward's room on the second floor.

He knocked and a woman's voice bade him enter, and in the lamplight he saw the whiteness of the bed linen and the greyness of Ward's face and the golden sheen of Celia's hair.

Awkwardly, Will came in as the girl beckoned and Ward's head turned slowly towards the ramrod.

'I'm glad you've shown up, Will,' he said slowly and with an effort. 'Reckon I'll be out of the runnin' for some time…'

'Phil tells me it was that goddam' grulla, Ward. Why in the hell were you crazy enough to ride it?'

A wan smile tiptoed across Ward Cabot's lined face. 'Just downright orneriness, Will, I guess. Maybe every one of us has got an unreasoning streak of obstinacy deep down somewhere inside.'

Will carefully rolled a cigarette and lit it without bothering even to glance at Celia Owen. He straddled a chair near the bed and laid his arms across its back, and as though in answer to his wondering, Ward spoke again.

'Celia came over with the doc at a moment's notice, Ward. She's been wonderful, the way she's looked after me.'

Will nodded. Mention of the doctor reminded him that one of the boys would have to ride for town and ask Laurie to call on Mike, at the Slash M.

'We'll carry on with the trail-herd for Brand City, Ward?' Will said presently.

The Stirrup owner nodded. 'Phil's kept up to schedule while you've been away ... reckon maybe we'll have a good herd ready by the week-end. What happened at Clear Fork?'

Will's sober glance found Celia Owen's face before shifting to Ward's.

'Quite a bit, Ward. I saw Paula–'

'How is she?' the older man interrupted with barely concealed eagerness.

Will said truthfully: 'She looks as beautiful as ever. Now I think I'll try and get her over to see you. Mike and I had reckoned on going to Clear Fork again, anyway; something to do with rustled beef. Just a few.'

Ward Cabot brushed that aside.

'You figure you could get Paula over here, Will? To come and see me?'

Kermody said: 'It's not that she isn't willing, Ward. She'd have come before. She'd have written more often. Ben's a – well, he's meaner than a thirst-crazed steer!'

Cabot nodded slowly and the girl said: 'I think he's getting tired now, Will. I figure he ought to rest now. I want to get him settled for the night.'

Kermody inclined his head, allowing that as Celia was the nurse, her word should be law with regard to her patient.

At the door he murmured for her to come outside on to the landing, and wonderingly she obeyed.

'I didn't aim to add to Ward's troubles, Celia,' Will said, 'but Mike got shot in Clear Fork. He isn't bad hurt though, thanks to some timely first aid. Maybe later tomorrow, if you get a chance, you could ride over and cheer him up?'

Will met her gaze unflinchingly, knowing that she would see through this thin artifice. Mike was crazy about Celia, but was too reticent to mention it or even show it. He backed away in her presence, at least when there were other folks about. Perhaps if he were alone with Celia for a while, he might find sudden strength and courage.

Yet, in spite of the girl's apparent disinterest, Will Kermody felt that if these two people could forget themselves and their fears and prejudices for a while, they might quite well plumb the hidden depths in themselves and rediscover each other.

Celia's glance dropped first. She seemed suddenly embarrassed that Will might read the aching desire in her gaze. With an effort she put her thoughts to the wounded Mike Lannigan, the man whom she thought was too crude and uncouth. Suddenly she looked up and her eyes were clear. 'I'll go and see him, Will,' she said quietly. 'If that's what you want.'

Kermody had to be content to leave it like that. She might yet get around to liking Mike. In any case there were more important things to see to. Get the doc to go out to Slash M tomorrow. See Phil about the cutting out and branding and move the trail-herd beef down to home pastures, ready for the drive to Brand City.

Ben Mackinnon smiled to himself as he considered how fast had been his mental reaction to Will Kermody's suggestions and with what speed he had acted.

Knowing, of course, that Selby Lynn had rented a room at the Golden Dollar and knowing, in spite of his evasive answers to Kermody, that Lynn was after cheap beef, and, therefore, rustled beef, he had immediately sought out Selby and made his suggestions.

He had told Lynn that they could fix up details later that night. Now this had been done and Selby and another man, Brad Killigrew, would take as much beef as Ben could supply, within reason, and no questions asked, provided the price was right.

A wicked satisfaction rode Ben as he thought of the humour of all this. Will Kermody had suggested that he, Ben, was rustling Pilgrim Valley beef. *Yet at that time the thought had not entered Mackinnon's head!*

He had been busy enough scraping up money to buy the Golden Dollar from Bull Chandler, wheedling, threatening and using everything in the book and some things that were not there.

At last he had succeeded and since Ben had brought Laura and his wife into the picture, the takings had soared to unprecedented levels.

Mackinnon, like all his kind, was smart enough to see that men who sweated all day and half the night in their desperate search for gold would require that much more in the way of liquor and entertainment to offset the crazy fever of their labours.

No one yet had struck a main seam or a mother lode, but there was enough promise of things to come in the gold dust panned from the creeks and the occasional trickles of ore turned over by shovel and pick. Enough to encourage the existing men to stay and even induce newcomers to ride in from time to time and catch the fever which condemned them to stay more surely than any quarantine restrictions.

Ben smiled again. There were other saloons in Clear Fork, but only one Golden Dollar. Only one Ben Mackinnon and only one (or should he say two?) of Paula and Laura!

Things were going fine right enough and now Kermody had come along and thrown the thing right into his lap without knowing it.

If Ben Mackinnon was going to be

accused of rustling when he was innocent, *then by God he'd cash in on it and become guilty*!

Apart from the growing demand in Clear Fork for butchered meat with no tell-tale hides attached, this gent Selby Lynn and his associate Brad What's-his-name would buy in fairly large quantities. And in the same way that Laura Paramour's mind had leaped ahead, so had Ben Mackinnon's, perhaps even more quickly.

He was going to rustle from his father-in-law. That meant he was virtually robbing his wife! The thought gave him no little sadistic pleasure.

But, if Ward died suddenly, the ranch would be Paula's. Why trouble then about rustling? All he need do was to send Nick Flore to await the right moment and then, after the ranch was Paula's, he could say: 'My dear, I need five hundred head of steers to sell to So-and-so. You must leave me to fix the price.' And Paula would give that goddam' hang-dog look and try her old tricks of letting the tears start so that her eyes were bright and wring those beautiful hands of hers in anguish – but it would make no difference. He would have his way just the same.

Yet, even in Pilgrim Valley, murder, stark and unprovoked, might not be so easy to cover up. True Nick Flore would take the rap, but he might also talk a lot before he swung.

Suppose therefore, he, Ben, let Ward Cabot stay safe and sound for a while. He still had a good enough crew, with perhaps another two or three added to help himself to the beef, and supposing they caught him? What then? Ward would never dare to press charges. Ben would force Paula to say they had been cut out with her knowledge and sanction and Ward would have to play it like Paula said. Ben even chuckled out loud as he thought of all this. Now he could start in earnest to make some money and begin buying up saloons and stores in Clear Fork. He would be a big man one day in this territory. Maybe the Governor even...

Downstairs, in the crowded, boisterous saloon, Art Millar had also been doing some heavy thinking.

He had not been too pleased with Ben of late. Ben, it seemed, was trying to ease him out. There had been no business deals recently which Millar could cash in on, and even in rip-roarin' Clear Fork the number of folk who wanted a highly paid gunman was disappointingly low!

But the thing which needled Art Millar most of all was the bitter pill he had been forced to swallow at the hands of the big Stirrup ramrod. Not once, but twice, and no man did a thing like that to Art Millar twice running and got away with it!

Instinctively Millar's big, bony hand slid to the black gun at his thigh whilst his left hand reached for his glass. He was barely conscious of the sea of faces in front of him and the swirl of drifting smoke. He was seeing again that lean, mocking face and feeling in imagination the shattering blow to the jaw which Kermody had dealt him at their first meeting. But far worse than that were the calculated insults which the ramrod had thrown in his teeth. Kermody would be dead by now, Millar swore, if Ben hadn't chipped in like that and laid his gunsights at the table.

Millar was near to sweating with suppressed anger as he thought back on all this, and it was several moments before he realized that Belle, one of the girls, was leaning her shapely arms on the table and talking to him.

'Wake up, Art!' She had to raise her harsh voice against the din as well as to pierce the wall of thought which shut off Art Millar's conscious mind from his surroundings.

He blinked a couple of times and growled an oath. 'God-dammit, Belle!' he snarled. 'Don't sit their mouthing at me. Spit it out for—'

'I been tryin' to tell you, jug-head,' she spat, 'for the last quarter-hour, an' ef'n you'd got any grey matter between them jug-handles you call ears, you'd know what I was talkin' about!'

'Stow that gab,' Millar growled again, thereby betraying something of his earlier life. 'I was thinkin' of somethin', Belle. Here, have a drink an' tell me what it is!'

Somewhat mollified, the girl poured herself a stiff dose and downed it at a single gulp.

She leaned forward, engulfing Millar in a wave of liquor, sweat and cheap perfume.

'Ben wants to see you, *pronto*,' she said. 'He's in the upstairs office. Better rustle, Art.'

She threw him an arch look and moved from the table with a swing of her hips.

Millar's gaze followed her provocative movements and then, roughly, he shouldered his way through the press of people and ascended the staircase to the floor above.

He crossed the landing and knocked on Ben's door, neither furtively nor loudly.

He entered in response to Mackinnon's yell and, as always, felt a surge of jealousy, an almost savage antagonism, against this suave, big man who always managed to get others to do the dirtiest chores.

Mackinnon studied the man even though his bold gaze moved with paradoxical casualness over Art Millar's bruised face. He knew what Art was thinking, more or less, and when he spoke it was with the characteristic pointedness that he always used to subordinates or lesser individuals.

'Kermody made quite a mark on your jaw, Art,' Ben said, and the sting in the words was washed cool by Mackinnon's easy smile.

Even so, anger flooded redly into Art's swarthy cheeks. 'Yes, Ben! And Kermody would be daid right now with no more cheap sneers and dirty insults ef'n you hadn't poked that gun at me. Why in hell didn't you let me finish him – or do you like him?'

Ben selected a cigar from the humidor on his desk and motioned to Millar to be seated.

He cut the cigar and lit it with a sulphur match, drawing on it until the lighted tip drew evenly. *To glow evenly*, Ben smiled to himself, *like his own thoughts*.

'You underrate Will Kermody, Art,' he said mildly, 'if you think he would be dead by now but for me. I think it might have been the other way about.'

'You crazy, Ben? My hand was a bare inch away from my gun. Both of Kermody's were hooked in his belt. I could have shot fust an' and then shot again–'

'Don't be a bigger fool than you need be, Art,' Mackinnon said with the faintest trace of a rasp in his rich voice. 'Have you ever seen Will Kermody draw and fire a pistol?'

Millar's big head moved from side to side. 'No, but–'

'There ain't any "buts", Art. It's the fastest thing I've ever seen, and the most deadly. *The fastest thing I've ever seen,*' he repeated, 'and there were seven hundred men in our Company when I was a captain.'

Art shrugged. Anger had given way to sulkiness. 'You think what you like, Ben.'

'I don't think, dam' you, Art. *I know*! But that's not what I wanted to talk to you about. You'll have your chance at Kermody at the right time and the right place! Listen. Here's where you start earning some of that money you get, and bonuses as well, no doubt. Before the end of the week, we'll be moving a hundred head of Stirrup beef and you'll be in charge of the detail.'

Mackinnon could not completely rid himself of the habit of using military terms occasionally.

'Kermody's stuff, eh, Ben?' Millar said and licked his lips.

'Don't let your natural dislike of the man blind you to the fact that Stirrup – so far – is Ward Cabot's, and Paula Cabot is my wife. I don't want any come-backs on this, Art, and if we can do it quietly and you can pull the boys *and* the cattle out, without shootings and killings, there should be good pickings for us for a long time to come.'

'Cripes,' Art said. 'I hadn't thought of it like that. About Mrs. Mackinnon, I mean, She's allus been, well' – Millar smiled ingratiatingly now that the prospects ahead were again rosy – 'Mrs. Mackinnon, I guess!'

Ben nodded, realizing again that Art's thought processes were not so fast as his triggering. Mackinnon waited for questions.

'How do we know where to find that much beef all in one place?' Art Millar said presently. He grinned. 'I reckon we won't have the time to round up one hun'erd head one at a time!'

'They're cutting out and rounding up beef right now,' Mackinnon smiled, 'ready to start a trail-drive to Brand City. As far as we know they won't start out *before* the week-end.

'My information is that there are upwards of a thousand steers, beef and cow critturs, close-herded near the ranch. Kermody and Cabot usually cut out almost a thousand for the spring drive to Brand City. That means you can pick a hundred or so easily, possibly even without attracting any attention.'

'There'll be night-riders?'

'Probably one-two, but only to see that the cattle doesn't wander back to the river by night. You've seen a thousand head of cattle at night, Art?'

Millar nodded. 'Sure. Back in Montany–'

'You know, then,' Ben cut in, 'that it would take a big crew to watch over that lot!'

Again the gunman nodded, but a puzzled expression crept into his eyes. 'How you know all this, Ben? Kin we rely on this info? Supposin' it's a trap?'

'There's no trap, Art, and my information comes straight from the fountain head.'

He did not see fit to tell Millar that soon after Kermody had left the Golden Dollar to return to the Bar 52, this same night, Fay Murphy, who carried a long-standing chip on his shoulder, had ridden on a lathered horse and had spoken to Ben and had been well paid. Particularly well paid, Mackinnon thought with a grin, because the information about the trail-herd and the bunched cattle had dove-tailed beautifully with Ben's new-born decision to 'go in for beef' in a big way!

Mackinnon remembered well how the taciturn Fay Murphy had nursed his grievance against Ward Cabot and Will Kermody when both men had made Murphy crawl and eat dirt for ill-treating a horse.

He had not been given his time for various reasons. The crew was short-handed and Cabot, after his initial upsurge of anger, had reverted to his easy-going attitude.

Kermody was prepared to forget the incident because Murphy had been punished and normally he was a good man at his job.

Ben smiled as he recollected some of the past and present situations at Stirrup. What Kermody did not realize was that Fay Murphy was the type of man who would never forget a thing like that, and in Jim Stewart Murphy had found a twin malcontent.

Once or twice before, Murphy had cunningly offered Ben tit-bits of useful information and had been paid well enough to share the proceeds with Stewart.

Thus it was that Stewart was a cast-iron alibi for Fay, and Murphy could do this night-ride in the full knowledge that, as far as Stirrup was concerned, both he and Jim were at the eastern line-cabin.

How Murphy had picked up this news at such distance from the home buildings, Ben had not asked. It was apparent that the man knew what he was talking about and was quite willing to forgo half his payment until the thing had been proved.

Assuming, therefore, that Ben's night crew found things as Fay had described, he would receive another fifty dollars for himself and Jim Stewart. Each would receive in all fifty dollars, the equivalent of a month's pay without work!

All in all, Ben considered that the whole thing was too good a bet to pass up.

Selby wanted beef; Kermody had almost accused Ben of rustling; Fay Murphy had brought specific information, and if anything went wrong, all Ben would have to do would be to dangle Paula before the eyes of Stirrup, in the belief that both Ward and Kermody would be powerless to act for fear of hurting her. What Ben had not considered was the other angle. That Will might act to *free* Paula!

CHAPTER 8

'YOU DONE SHOT THE MARSHAL!'

Will Kermody glanced at the clock in the hall as he came down from Ward Cabot's room. The hands pointed to twenty after seven.

Will became aware that his belly felt empty, and came out on to the veranda to find Phil Hankins hovering in the shadows.

'I'm going back to Clear Fork, Phil. Going to try and bring Paula back to see the old man.'

'*Tonight?*' Hankins's voice raised itself a notch in surprise.

Will nodded. 'Just as soon as I can conjure something to eat out of Chuck!

'Get someone to ride to town and ask the doc to call at the Slash M tomorrow, Phil.'

Hankins said: 'Tim's done a deal of riding lately. The others are still eating. I'll go myself.'

Will tromped down the steps and walked slowly across the yard to the bunk-house and cook-shack.

Brec Chase and Dave Swallow were just finishing their coffee. Sid Vincent and young Furnival were still eating.

Chuck turned from the stove and saw the foreman.

'Howdy, Will. Take a pew and I'll rustle you up some grub.'

'Thanks, Chuck,' Kermody said, and turned to the room in general.

'Bad news about the boss.'

Brec Chase nodded his big head.

'That goddam' grulla! Both Phil and young Tim tried to keep Ward off'n its back but he wouldn't listen—'

'It's a lousy shame Miss Paula's not still here,' Sid Vincent grunted, looking up from his plate.

'I'm going to fetch her,' Kermody said quietly, taking his place on the long bench at the table.

'It's a long pull,' Dave Swallow objected. 'You only jest done got back from Clear Fork, ain't you, Will?'

'Yes, but I'm taking a fresh mount and I'll kill it to Zach Keeler's and swop for something alive!'

The men grinned and Chuck Anderson let out a low, rumbling laugh as he waddled forward with a plate of hot steak heaped with beans, tomatoes and fried potatoes.

They all knew that Kermody could get more out of a horse than anyone else. He was like a damned Injun for that. Somehow, in spite of his weight and size, he could nurse along a lame or jaded mount where others would have to admit failure.

In any case, they all knew that Will would not go even close to killing his mount. He loved horses too much for that, and if he was going to take the stage road and swap mounts at the trading post, instead of cutting across the range, he'd make good time without injuring either the Stirrup pony or Zach Keeler's.

Will steadily applied himself to the task of eating as the men drifted through to the bunk-house. He set to figuring how he would play this thing. Whether it would be worth making an issue of it in the case of any interference from Ben.

Suppose Ben dug in his heels and said simply, 'Paula's not going, Will'? Would it be worth while drawing a gun and fighting it out?

Kermody grinned a little as he mentally chided himself for running too far ahead. He'd play the cards the way they fell. If it came to a showdown, he'd decide then what to do. Maybe he could engineer this quietly. Maybe Ben would be back at the ranch some place and he could see Paula alone.

He pushed back the tin plate and Chuck Anderson came forward with a huge wedge of pie.

Will murmured his quiet appreciation and proceeded to do ample justice to Chuck's pastry-making.

The cook beamed down at him. Will, he thought, could always be relied upon to appreciate any trouble that a body took whether it was cooking or anything else. But especially cooking. The woman who landed the Stirrup foreman would have to be more than an ordinary cook, Chuck Anderson told himself, if they were to stay happily united.

'I've heated some water, Will,' the cook said, pouring out a cup of coffee. 'Figgered you wouldn't wanta go washin' at the pump by lantern light!'

Kermody had almost forgotten the trail-dust which still clung to his face and hands and powdered his hair and clothes.

He thanked the cook and rose, stripping off calf-skin vest, shirt and under-vest.

He sluiced himself in the warm, suddy water and rubbed himself briskly with a towel taken from the locker beside his bunk.

Fatigue fell away from him as he shrugged into a clean shirt and an old sweater. He combed back the long, wet, reddish-brown hair and replaced the black, low-crowned stetson.

Tim came in from the yard poking his head round the door.

'Phil's lit out fer town, Will, an' I got your rig on the white-stockinged buckskin.'

'Good man,' Will said. 'You put my carbine in the boot?'

'Sure,' Tim Furnival grinned, 'an' they's dried meat an' crackers in your saddle-bags as well as extry shells an' a fresh canteen of water!'

Kermody knew a sudden surge of feeling – of well-being. Here at Stirrup, men thought of these things. Maybe he was spoiled. Who could say? Yet it was the sort of spoiling which did no harm to a man.

The looking to such things as grub and water and guns and a good horse had many a time saved a man's life. Perhaps, after all, these things were not symbols of spoiling or luxury. They were necessities when it came to riding away from the warm, comforting protection and strength of the ranch. Will knew, in that sudden moment of intro-spection, that there were many things here at Stirrup that he would not find in other places if he should ever leave this spread.

Then the thought came to him, too, as it had done to some of those in Clear Fork. His mind had switched to Ward, the owner, lying up there helpless in bed.

What would happen if Ward died? *The ranch would be Paula's!* More likely, he considered bleakly, it would be Paula's in name only and handled and managed by Ben Mackinnon.

The thought was a chilly one on which to depart from the cosy warmth of the cook-shack.

'See that Miss Owen has whatever she wants, Tim,' Will called as he hit leather, and grinned as he caught the roan flush on young Furnival's face revealed by the lamplight from the open bunk-house door.

Will Kermody even *looked* like an Injun when he rode really fast.

The stars were out with the bright moon and Stirrup's foreman knew every inch of the terrain even before striking the stage road.

He leaned forward in the stirrups, plumb-lining his weight across the pony's withers, holding the reins lightly but short, yet allowing the well-bred buckskin all the play it needed.

When they hit the stage road, Kermody crouched lower in the stock saddle. Knees were sharply bent now and body hunched forward towards the buckskin's flying mane.

The cool, sage-scented night air rushed by, plucking at clothes and hair and rawhide strings.

This trip would have been unnecessary if Will had arrived back Monday night instead of Tuesday. Then, Jack Taylor, the stage-driver, could have taken a note to Paula, giving it first into the hands of Laura Paramour. But the stage had left this morning for Clear Fork and would not return until Friday.

Perhaps, after all, a note would not have sufficed. No one would know until much later whether or not Paula had received it.

This way, Will could ascertain the situation first hand. Either Paula would be allowed to come or else, if Ben was about, he might perhaps raise obstacles.

The question of Paula seeing her father was not desperately urgent in itself. Ward was not dying, and according to Doc Laurie, was in no danger.

Rather was this going to be a battle of wills; one man reserving the right to demand that his wife did as he said, the other, nudging, prodding, grinning and perhaps even testing the incredibly fast and accurate draw of Ben Mackinnon!

So Will's thoughts rode with him in that flying night-ride across the floor of Pilgrim Valley.

Twice he drew rein and gave the lathered and hard-breathing buckskin a blow, and the second time he was a bare three miles from Zach Keeler's post...

Will clattered into the yard in a cloud of swirling dust and flying gravel. Dirt and sweat streaked both rider and horse. Will glanced at the moon, figuring out the time taken.

He had eaten at seven-thirty and had left just after eight. It was roughly forty miles to this half-way stage, by road, and now Kermody considered the westering moon and put the time at somewhere between ten and ten-thirty o'clock.

He slid from the hull as the door of the 'dobe building opened. Zach Keeler stood half concealed by the heavy door, a long-barrelled Colt dangling from his hand.

'It's Will Kermody, Zach,' the Stirrup ramrod called, and the gross-looking horse-trader relaxed.

'Light down an' eat, Will,' Keeler commanded in his thick, wheezy voice. 'We'll see to the horse presently.'

Kermody trailed the reins and left the buckskin within reach of the half-filled trough of water, where it drank greedily and noisily.

He followed Keeler into the post and was aware of the man's close scrutiny.

Zach Keeler was in shirt-sleeves and braces, sleeves rolled up to reveal thick, hairy arms. He wore waist overalls and run-down cowboots and a wide, leather belt acted as surcingle for his big, swaying paunch.

He was nearly bald and a two-day stubble sprouted from his dark, quivering jowls.

Now he waddled through an inner room to the kitchen and set coffee on to boil. Again he fixed Will with his bright, enquiring gaze.

'Just coffee, Zach,' Kermody said. 'And a good horse. I'll be on my way again in a few minutes.'

The fat man grunted and moved his gaze from Kermody's face to his dusty clothes.

Kermody knew no reason why this man should not have an explanation, so he gave it.

'I'm riding to Clear Fork tonight, Zach. Ward's been thrown from a horse, and I figured it was about time Paula came over, anyway.'

'Mrs. Mackinnon?'

'Yes,' Will said drily. 'Mrs. Ben Mackinnon.'

'Why the break-neck pace, Will?' Keeler asked, pouring sweetened milk into two thick mugs.

Will rolled and lit a smoke. 'We're in the middle of round-up, for one thing. I've already been away from Stirrup since Sunday.'

Zach Keeler sank into a rocker, his heavy body almost over-flowing the seat and arms.

'Got a good bay colt, Will. Four-year-old. Not long gentled, but it'll git you anywhere to hell-an-breakfast in a hurry! I'll git a lantern an' throw your rig on the bay.'

They both drank the warming coffee and smoked cigarettes and presently Zach lumbered to his feet again and lit a storm lantern. He shuffled to the rear door with Will following on behind.

Kermody knew well the lay-out of covered barns, the long stables, wherein was housed some of the finest horse-flesh in the country.

The yard was straw- and manure-littered and a man had to watch his step walking from the 'dobe-house to the nearest of the mud-and-timber outbuildings.

Will followed the bobbing light ahead as Zach's vast bulk disappeared from view into the interior of the nearest barn.

Here, the sharp ammonia-scented air, the pungent odour of leather and horse-sweat, stung the nostrils, yet pleasantly for men such as these.

Zach led the way past the stalls, and as Will lengthened his stride, coming quickly nearer, something caught his eyes. Something that had for a moment come within the moving yellow arc of lamplight.

Will had even gone on a few paces before he pulled up in mid-stride, his mind only now just absorbing what his eyes had already glimpsed.

He went back to the stall and gave the sorry-looking paint pony a long, measuring look. Close to, even away from Zach's lantern, he made out the Stirrup brand on rump and shoulder. He had wanted to make sure. Some brands could be mistaken for others in the semi-darkness or at a considerable distance. He was not mistaken. That was Fay Murphy's horse!

Thoughtfully Kermody came up to where Zach was leading a beautiful bay colt by a rope halter.

Without a word, Keeler passed the rope to Will and the ramrod led the way back to the yard.

'I'll go and bring your mount round,' Zach grunted as he ambled round the side of the house and returned moments later with the jaded buckskin.

Will took off the bridle and placed it over the colt's head while Zach fumbled and grunted with the cinch straps of the stock saddle.

Presently, the rig aboard the restlessly pawing colt, both men straightened up and looked at each other in the moonlight.

Zach pulled a flask from his overalls and passed the bottle across to the Stirrup man and Will downed some of the liquor gratefully. It was warming to the stomach against the coldness of the night.

'Good stuff, Zach,' he grunted, returning the bottle, and then added quietly:

'What's Fay Murphy been doing here?'

Keeler chuckled and his fat jowls quivered grotesquely in the eerie moon- and starlight.

He gulped down a good-size drink and wiped his mouth with the back of a blackened, hairy hand.

'Wondered if you'd notice that, Will. Say, thar ain't much wrong with yore eyesight. C'm on inside. You kin ground-tie the bay. He won't budge.'

Back in the kitchen Will surveyed the hostler in silence. He knew that Zach would not be hurried in parting with information. This sort of thing was one of the small, savouring pleasures of a lonely and generally uneventful life.

'Murphy comes ridin' hell-fer-leather on – when was it? – Monday night. Yep, last night that was. Seems longer ago'n that.

'Guess he didn't figger you'd have any cause to visit old man Zach's tradin' post.'

'Why, Zach, I guess not. It's been some long time since I've called in here to yarn or swop a horse.'

Keeler's dark, fat head nodded, setting off the loose cheeks and dewlaps into another quivering dance.

'I kinda got the impression he didn't want anyone at Stirrup to know about this, Will, 'specially you.'

'He's supposed to be line-riding with Jim Stewart fifty miles from here,' Will said mildly.

'He told me to keep a blanket on the paint. Said it got shivering fits. Well, I did keep it on until I saw you arrive tonight. When I went out back for the can of cawfee, I tweaked off that horse-blanket an' left the rest to you.'

'You can move mighty fast when you like, Zach. You weren't gone above a couple of minutes.

'You'd better take this for your trouble,' Will said, laying a twenty-dollar piece on the table. 'I might want to "buy" that horse.'

Both men grinned, understanding each other in their different ways.

Will had thought Zach would not be above taking a 'reward' for information given. After all, Stirrup's troubles were not Zach Keeler's. He could have kept quiet about it. Besides which he had traded his best horse; a far better mount than even the buckskin. Will did not begrudge the money for the information. He was beginning to wonder, now, about Fay Murphy and Jim Stewart.

He moved to the rear door and asked, 'What road was Fay taking, Zach?'

Keeler did not reply until both men were in the yard once more and Will was aboard

130

the plunging bay.

For a few moments his undivided attention was necessary until he had communicated his strength of mind, as well as hands and arms, to the colt's intelligence.

It was not long before the bucking and plunging was over and the bay responded eagerly to the hands and knees of its new boss.

'He was takin' the stage-trail to Clear Fork, Will. It's a wonder you didn't see him at the settlement!'

Kermody nodded and lifted his hand in salute. He trotted the bay round the side of the house and clattered across the front yard.

In a matter of moments he was low in the saddle, racing along the ragged moonlit trail to Clear Fork, the problem of Fay Murphy nudging at his mind.

Clear Fork was going full blast when Will Kermody turned the game but foam-flecked bay into the first livery he found.

He gave instructions to the hostler and paid some money in advance to ensure that the horse would be seen to properly.

Now he was here, Will wondered just what his first move should be.

He ascended the board-walk on the Golden Dollar side, and rolled a cigarette, his gaze moving along the noisy street.

Somewhere at the other end of Main a pistol cracked and Will heard the shrill scream of the slug before it buried itself somewhere in the dark shadows. Bursts of laughter followed, giving evidence that this was merely an hilarious wolf whose night it was to howl.

Kermody had lit his cigarette carefully. He was on the alert for trouble. This was a young, lusty and uninhibited mushroom town, and apart from drunks and bullies, Will remembered that at least two men might be after his blood. Certainly Art Millar and, possibly, even Charlie Ridewell, the thin and rangy, tough marshal.

It was, Will judged, somewhere around twelve-thirty and the narrow plank-walks were still crowded enough to make walking difficult, the more so as more than a few burly, bearded miners were weaving uncertain courses and often half stumbling into the dirt.

One such figure lurched against Will, half pushing him to one side and, as Kermody reached for the man's shoulder to swing him round, he felt the unmistakable prod of a six-gun's barrel pushing hard against his left ribs.

He turned back now, slowly and quietly, away from the stumbling miner and found himself looking into the brown leather face of Marshal Ridewell.

There was a strange bitterness in that face, Kermody saw, even in the uncertain light of the plank-walk. As though Ridewell's consuming hatred of the world in general was now turned with all its savage force and intensity on to one man.

Perhaps Ridewell was tired of spending his life sitting in the pockets of such men as Ben Mackinnon. Perhaps there was some other reason for this bitter mood so plainly revealed in the man's bright eyes and in the shape of the thin, drawn-down mouth behind the stained moustaches.

Will couldn't figure it, but he did sense that right now he wouldn't give much for his chances. Ridewell was trigger-happy sure enough and Kermody stood still, and then the whisky fumes hit him full in the face.

'I thought I told you to clear out by sundown, bucko,' Ridewell said in the thinnest of voices. 'You seem to be a pilgrim as doesn't take kindly to advice!'

'I spent last night at Ben Mackinnon's spread,' Will said mildly, 'and returned to Pilgrim Valley this afternoon–'

'Then what happened?' Ridewell sneered. 'You develop wings?'

The Stirrup man said: 'Something came up. I had to come back here so I changed horses at Zach Keeler's–'

'*Hey, Charlie!*' A man's sudden shout came from across the street and for a thought-flash the marshal's attention was divided. In that briefest moment of time, Will felt the gun ease away from his ribs and before Ridewell could re-focus his mind to the Stirrup ramrod, Kermody's iron grip had descended on Ridewell's wrist, twisting it with sudden and violent force so that the gun was no longer pointed at his middle.

The marshal's finger, either purposely or involuntarily, tightened on the trigger and the roar of the Walker Colt sounded deafeningly loud.

Will's long, right arm was now squeezing the marshal's bony body as his left hand sought to deflect the gun still further from him.

Ridewell's gun-hand was forced slowly back by the irresistible strength of Will's grip.

Kermody was vaguely conscious of blurred faces watching; of rough voices shouting advice to the two contestants. Beyond all that was the knowledge that Ridewell was fighting like a crazy drunk and that if he could turn that gun and fire, there would be no stopping him.

Ridewell's boot hacked at Will's shin and then his knee came up to the crotch, but Kermody had been half-expecting that and the sickening jolt was taken by his turning hip. He squeezed harder with his left hand and turned the gun further, and then another deafening report rolled out and acrid smoke drifted up to Will's wide nostrils and suddenly Ridewell's figure was as slack as a sack of wheat.

The next moment he was on the planks, blood slowly staining his shirt where the vest had fallen open.

Kermody controlled his laboured breathing with an effort and turned to a man in the crowd.

'Better get him into his office and fetch a doctor–'

'Sure,' the man said and weaved a way through the throng.

'What happened, brother?' a big miner asked, and then added naïvely, 'You done shot the marshal!'

Kermody faced the speaker and there was something in the ramrod's face that cut off any protests or angry denunciations from the crowd.

'He threw a gun on me,' Will said coldly. 'He was crazy drunk, and if he dies it's his own damned fault!'

Then Kermody moved and men dropped back, allowing him a free and unhindered passage as he walked down-street, and turned into the hell-roarin' Golden Dollar.

CHAPTER 9

TEMPORARY FREEDOM

The news carried ahead, somehow, as it always does, and Will knew this the moment he entered the noisy, smoke- and laughter-laden atmosphere of the Golden Dollar.

Not that there was any sudden and dramatic silence. It was just that the noise and uproar slipped down a few notches and men's glances shuttled across to Kermody's high figure as he made for the bar.

Ray Clarke's beady gaze was bright, with an almost malicious gleam of satisfaction.

The shot glass of whisky was produced with the air of a conjuror and Will smiled and paid out another gold piece, not for the drink; this was payment for the future. Maybe there might be a time when Will would be glad to know that the scatter-gun under Ray Clarke's counter would not be directed at his back...

'We heerd you shot the marshal, Kermody. That right?'

Will rolled a smoke and lit it.

'He threw a gun on me, Ray. I pushed it

away. I guess you could say Ridewell shot himself!'

Clarke grinned, showing broken teeth. He evidently had no more love for the marshal than he had for Art Millar.

'Where's Ben?' the ramrod asked.

'Up in his room, or in Miz M'kinnon's,' the bartender said.

Will's glance travelled up to the gallery on whose further side several doors were visible across the landing.

'Which one, Ray?'

Clarke leaned forward across the bar counter. 'For God's sake don't tell him I told you, Kermody. He don't take kindly to folks interruptin' him. His upstairs office is the third one from the head of the stairs. Miz M'kinnon's room is beyond.'

'Don't worry, Ray. I won't bring you into this,' Will grunted.

He crossed to the foot of the stairs and took his time ascending, wondering at Ben's terrific power over such as Ray Clarke. He realized more than ever now the savage ruthlessness that lay close beneath the surface of Ben's suave and smiling veneer.

He heard voices raised in angry argument and the sound of a scuffle and a half-sob, followed by the sharp, whip-like crack of a flat hand hitting flesh.

Will grimly figured this was the right room and turned the handle without bothering to knock.

Paula was pressed back against a big sofa and Ben's hand was raised to strike again. Even from that distance Will could see the white marks on her face where his hand had hit.

He hooked thumbs in gun-belt, grinding down the anger that threatened to send him flying for Ben's throat, and slammed the door with his foot.

Mackinnon wheeled. 'Haven't I told–' he began in a roaring voice, then stopped as he recognized the completely relaxed figure of the Stirrup ramrod.

'Sorry if I'm butting in, Ben,' Will said mildly. 'I wanted to see you both, anyway. Howdy, Paula,' he said to the girl, and removed his hat, carefully, with his left hand.

Mackinnon's face was flushed with anger and drink. For all his usual suavity he could not recover himself as quickly as his wife did.

'What's the idea, Will?' Ben's voice held a rasp. 'Don't you ever knock on doors? Particularly in another man's house?'

'Why, Ben, I knew it was the right room, because I heard your voice,' Will smiled easily. 'If it had been anyone else but you, I would have said the voice was shouting.

'Maybe,' Will went on, 'it's just because this matchboarding's so blamed thin. It's really surprising what you can hear on the outside.'

'Since when have you been an eaves-dropper, Will?' Ben sneered, straightening his coat and cravat and striving hard to push down the lid on his temper.

'You should know me better than that, Ben,' Will said softly, and added wickedly: 'I don't *have* to eavesdrop. Folk tell me things. I'm what they call *receptive*. Like when I was told Fay Murphy came here last night when he should have been over seventy miles away at the line-cabin!'

Kermody had purposely used the word 'here', so as to cover Clear Fork or the Golden Dollar itself. Ben would have no way of knowing to which Kermody was referring.

A dull roan flush spread itself over Mackinnon's face, and again Will saw that bright spark of apprehension, or something near to it, in the dark, bold eyes.

With a supreme effort that was visible to both Will and Paula, Ben harnessed his temper and sat down at his desk, reaching into the humidor for a cigar.

When it was cut and lit, and drawing evenly, he leaned back, miraculously composed now.

'Fay Murphy, *here*, Will? He's one of your riders, isn't he?'

Will nodded. He had slung his hat on the floor and was now straddling an upright chair in his usual fashion. He noticed Ben's glance touch the butt of the six-gun in its holster on Will's thigh.

'Well, I suppose there's no law that says a man cain't ride into Clear Fork–'

'Marshal Ridewell seemed to think so, Ben,' Will said softly.

'Ridewell? Oh yes. You had a run in with him the other day.' Ben smiled. 'I guess he only told you to report to him. It's my orders, Will, you see. We don't encourage drifters.'

Kermody grinned wickedly. 'I wasn't referring to my "run-in" with him, as you call it, on Monday. It was just now, Ben.' Will's voice was deceptively apologetic. 'You see, Ben, Ridewell kind of shot himself–'

'*What*!' Mackinnon roared, half rising from his chair.

'Look, Will, if you're being funny, it's got to stop, see? I reckon I don't allow–' Ben broke off suddenly as his mind groped for and found the odd point about all this.

'Say! What the hell are you doin' back here, Will? Didn't you light out for Pilgrim Valley before dawn this morning, along with Lannigan? *What's going on?*' Ben demanded. *'Why have you come back?'*

'That's what I'm trying to get around to,' Kermody drawled. 'Ward's been hurt – thrown from a horse. It's all right, Paula,' he went on, intercepting the girl's anxiously questioning glance. 'He's not bad hurt but

140

he wants to see you all the same–'

'How bad hurt?' It was Ben who got in with the question before the girl could speak.

'His left leg's broken. It'll be some time before he rides again, if at all.'

'That all?' Ben snorted. 'What's the rush for then, Will? Why this night-ride if he's in no danger?'

Will said: 'We're in the middle of round-up. I've already taken time off looking for stolen beef. I figured that by changing horses I could make good time and get Paula back before too much of tomorrow is wasted.'

'But Paula's needed here, Will,' Ben protested. 'She cain't leave on a pleasure trip. We're busy here. Just beginning to build up a business.'

'You got Laura,' Will pointed out. 'Guess she wouldn't mind taking Paula's turn for a coupla days, 'specially if you paid her well – out of the profits,' the ramrod finished pointedly.

'See here, Will,' Ben said, stabbing the air with his cigar in Kermody's direction. 'You run your cattle in Pilgrim Valley and leave me to run my business in Clear Fork. Paula's–'

'–going back with me,' Will finished quietly and the breathless, sticky silence was like a tangible yet invisible wall crowding in

141

on them in that room. Beyond that closed-in silence was the background of noise from downstairs and in the room itself the quiet ticking of an ormolu clock.

'Who says so?' Ben said softly.

Will's hard gaze came up and found Mackinnon's face. 'I hoped you'd see reason, Ben,' he said quietly. 'It hardly seems the sort of thing to warrant going for our guns. One of us most likely would be killed.'

Mackinnon's thick brows rose in genuine surprise. 'You mean you'd go for your gun and shoot me, Will, just because I told you to mind your own dam' business with regard to my wife?' There was a kind of shocked incredulity in his face. This man Kermody was a strange, as well as a tough, hombre.

Will nodded gently. Both Ben and Paula could see now that somehow Kermody's right hand had transferred itself from the back of the chair to his thigh, the movement having escaped them both. It was about four inches from the black-handled gun.

Ben blew out his cheeks and then laughed suddenly and loudly.

'Reckon you've been drinking kerosene, Will, and now you're going about looking for a match to set it off.

'It ain't worth making such an issue of, Will. We'd both be crazy. Take Paula back to see her old man tomorrow – tonight for all I care – but I tell you she'll have to be back by Friday. I cain't spare her longer than that!

'Now what's all this about Marshal Ridewell? You know, Will, if you ain't careful, someone's going to take a pot shot at you one of these days.'

Will smiled. 'It'll probably be at night-time, Ben.

'As to Ridewell, I guess he shot himself.' Kermody told the story briefly, succinctly, and Ben was forced to admit that he, Will, had at least some slight justification.

'But you cain't go about shooting duly elected law-men, Will, you know.' Ben's tone was one of admonishment. The tone one might adopt with a particularly difficult child.

'I don't crowd easy, Ben,' Will said softly.

Will Kermody gazed thoughtfully at the bay colt which had brought him lickety-spit from Zach Keeler's to Clear Fork.

For a horse that had travelled some forty-odd miles, mostly at a fast pace, it looked remarkably fresh, particularly as the hostler had fed and watered it and made a top-hand job of cleaning and brushing the coat. It was close to 2 a.m. and the old liveryman yawned loudly and without restraint as he held the lantern the better for Will's inspection.

Some folks, you'd think, hadn't got any

beds. Riding all this way to Clear Fork at night and then coming back a few hours later to see whether the hoss was fresh enough to ride back!

Dewey Ruskin, the hostler, so-called because of the permanent dew-drip which dangled from his protuberant nose at all times, hung the lantern on to a peg.

'Time I was locking up, mister,' he said, shuffling his feet.

Kermody dragged his gaze away from the bay and plunged a hand into his pocket, withdrawing the balance of the money due to the hostler – and a bit over the side.

'The gate's got a slip padlock on a hasp and staple,' Will said. 'I'll douse the lantern and close the door for you.'

For a moment the old man put his gaze over the tall, lean figure of the man from Pilgrim Valley, but was evidently satisfied with what he found.

He nodded his acceptance of this arrangement. He was so tired he felt he would have agreed to anything just so long as he could get to his bed in the adjoining shack. But even now this man detained him with a sudden crushing grip on his arm.

'Hold it, Ruskin,' Will said. 'I'll want a mount for Mrs. Mackinnon!' Dewey's brows lifted a fraction in tired surprise.

'To rent?' he said.

Will nodded. 'She'll ride it back from

Stirrup early Friday. I want something as good as the bay.'

Dewey Ruskin pointed to a stall close at hand wherein a paint pony stood, alert for all the late hour and with an intelligent and enquiring eye.

Will leaned over the top of the stall and ran an experienced eye over the well-built animal. It was slightly longer in the leg and broader in the chest than most cow-ponies, and appeared to possess that valuable and indispensable combination of speed and endurance.

Will nodded and paid the hire fee, leaving a substantial deposit for both horse and saddle. The latter he saw was also good and there was a tolerable bridle hanging from the wall.

When Will turned, the old man was shuffling away and Kermody smiled to himself. It had gotten around town, quickly enough, that the Pilgrim Valley man, the Stirrup ramrod, was pretty close to Ben Mackinnon.

That meant that it would be best to treat Kermody with the same respect and deference as that accorded to Ben.

Will doubted that anyone of the traders in Clear Fork would refuse any reasonable request that he should make. Until such time, of course, as Ben decided to declare open war!

Now Kermody moved into the stall talking to the paint gently and letting the animal get to know him.

After a while, he saddled and bridled the pony without any difficulty and began wondering about Paula.

He checked his own restlessness, knowing that he had been in the livery no more than fifteen or twenty minutes and realizing that Paula would have to change into her range clothes and maybe pack one or two personal items in a blanket roll.

He heard her step as he straightened up from the cinch-strap and turned to greet her, waiting until she should reach the radius of light cast by the hanging lantern.

'Will?' she said with a slight hesitancy and immediately Kermody realized that he himself was partly in shadow.

'Here, Paula.'

He had known that if he ever saw her like this, the old wounds would start throbbing, and yet the whole thing had built itself into this pattern, this shape, with no conscious thoughts in his mind of any clandestine night-meeting.

Yet that's how it seemed now, and Will felt curiosity tug at him as to how Paula herself would react.

She was dressed as she had always been when back at Stirrup, in a long, divided riding skirt and cow-boots, shirt-blouse and

146

low-crowned stetson.

But he was quick to notice that even in range-rig there was a subtle difference between the old Paula and the new one, even though, now, almost every trace of cosmetics had been washed from her face.

The lamplight limned her face and upper body as she joined him, and the breathless beauty of her was something to jolt a man out of his senses.

She had loosened the lustrous black hair and tied it with a single ribbon, so that it formed a black, shining frame to her rather pale face.

Almost with reluctance, his gaze left her face and swept over her young, supple figure in a warm look of admiration.

He took in the inadequate thinness of the blue-grey shirt-blouse, made suddenly aware of this by the rounded symmetry of her breasts.

'It's cold on the range at nights, Paula. Have you forgotten?'

He saw now the blanket roll that she carried and reached forward to take it.

'I've a coat in there, Will. I guess I didn't think. I was so scared – and relieved at the same time! Dammit to hell, Will,' she said, striving desperately to keep the sudden surge of tears from coursing down her cheeks, 'I thought Ben would kill you, back there in the office! There! Now you've heard me use language that no lady would ever use...' She bit her lips in vexation, not knowing whether to laugh or cry.

Kermody took her arms gently.

'Pull out of it, kid,' he grinned, 'and get that coat on. Reckon you haven't been out range-riding for quite a spell?'

'Not since I left Stirrup,' she said. 'Oh Will—'

She was in his arms, crying softly against his chest, and Kermody masked his own intense feelings with difficulty.

It was he who was the one to draw apart this time.

'Let's get going, Paula, and see if you've forgotten how to ride.'

His matter-of-fact casualness brought her back quickly to her surroundings.

In a few minutes she had withdrawn the short coat from the blanket roll and Will re-tied it, lashing it to the cantle with the raw-hide strings of the saddle-skirts.

He handed the paint's reins to the girl and fetched the already saddled bay, leading the way from the livery and blowing the lantern flame out, just inside the doorway.

He left the lamp on Dewey Ruskin's stool and led the horses out into the moonlight night, fixing the hasp and staple and snapping the padlock shut.

Will, watching for signs, saw Paula climb into leather like the old hand she was. The sight gave him a queer pleasure which he found difficult to analyse and understand.

In a moment or two they were thundering out of town like twin spirits released from earthly bondage and enjoying the spiritual ecstasy of that sudden-found freedom...

They held to the easy, mile-eating lope that comes so naturally to range-bred horses, until Will drew in to the side of the trail for a brief halt.

He released his right boot from the stirrup and swung his leg round the saddle-horn while his fingers shaped a cigarette.

Paula sat relaxed and easy in the saddle, her feet swinging clear of the stirrups. The moon was rolling down towards a low range of hills in the west, but she watched him quietly in such light as there was.

When the cigarette was glowing evenly, Paula spoke.

'I don't know how you managed to make Ben climb down, Will. No other man has ever done such a thing.'

Kermody blew smoke down his nostrils and smiled.

'Just a question of how far a man's prepared to go, Paula,' he said gently. 'Ben knew I wasn't kidding. He knew I was prepared to have a show-down. What he couldn't understand was why any hombre would be prepared to fight a gun-duel on such an issue.'

She nodded. 'Ben cain't figure you out, Will. I've seen that these last two days. I think you've got him worried.'

She was silent a moment, before adding, 'I guess, maybe, I cain't quite figure you out myself.'

Will turned his head and laid his gaze over her darkly etched face and her straight, supple figure.

'Why, Paula? What's so difficult to figure out?'

She tried to choose her words carefully. 'Why should any man be prepared to kill or be killed just because the other one might refuse to let his wife leave town for a day or two?

'It's almost as though you don't value your life any more. Make no mistake, Will, Ben's terribly fast with a gun. I think you might have been the one to go under.'

'Even so,' Kermody grinned, 'Ben wasn't prepared to put it to the test, was he?

'I'd already shaken him a little by barging in and then mentioning Fay Murphy and the shooting of Charlie Ridewell!'

Will suddenly stubbed out his cigarette on the saddle-horn and found stirrups.

'I reckon you ought to know how I felt last spring, Paula,' he said softly. 'It's just the same now, only more so! C'm on see if you can beat me to Zach Keeler's!'

CHAPTER 10

STRANGE PARTNERSHIP

At the trading post, both Will and Paula had slept exhaustedly, sitting upright in the chairs before the dying stove.

Well before dawn, Keeler was stirring, replenishing the stove with wood from the box and setting coffee to boil and bacon to fry.

Kermody washed up at the pump outside, leaving Paula to make her rough toilet in the kitchen.

By the time they had cleaned up, they were both ready to wolf the breakfast that Keeler had prepared.

It was still only a little after 6 a.m. when they were in the saddle again, Will now riding the rested Stirrup buckskin, in exchange for the bay.

The girl's paint, after its two-hour rest, was game enough to try and race the buckskin. And as the sun rose, bathing the range with its life-giving warmth and light, Paula Mackinnon felt a choking feeling in her throat and a smarting in her eyes, nor was it because of the yellow dust stirred by the

151

galloping hoofs of their ponies.

At about nine o'clock they topped the last rise in the trail before Stirrup and gazed down at the collection of trim buildings.

Will shot her a swift glance but Paula had her feelings more under control. She smiled back and gently raked the pony with her silver spurs.

Kermody followed and together they clattered into the yard, drawing up near the rack in a dust-raising halt.

Chuck Anderson looked out from the bunk-house and, identifying the riders, waved a hand and came hurrying up.

He was still sweaty from his exertions in the cook-shack, although Phil and Sid Vincent had long since ridden out. But Paula was too glad to see an old friend to mind or even notice.

She hugged him tightly and Chuck's plum face creased up in a kind of embarrassed happiness.

'It's good to see you again, Chuck,' Paula laughed. 'Why, you're putting on weight again.'

The cook grinned. 'It's sure good to see you, too, Miss Paula. Howdy, Will! Reckon you two want somethin' to eat.'

Kermody shook his head. 'We had breakfast at Zach's place, but I, for one, could go a cup of coffee–'

'Me, too,' Paula laughed. 'But first I must

go and see Dad.'

Anderson nodded. 'I'll make some fresh and bring it over to the gallery here.'

Will followed the girl up the veranda steps as Celia Owen came through the screen door.

'Hallo, Celia,' Paula greeted. 'How is Dad?'

'He's going along fine, Paula,' Celia said. 'I'd say he'll be even better after seeing you.'

Paula laughed and ran into the house, and Celia's puzzled gaze followed until she disappeared from sight.

The dressmaker's gaze came round and lifted to Will's face. The puzzled expression was still there in her eyes.

'She doesn't look like – like – what folks say,' Celia finished lamely.

Will's face was tight, even though he told himself that Celia's reaction would be that of most folks in Pilgrim Valley.

'There's more pure gold in Paula Cabot than in all the streams and creeks at Clear Fork,' Will said roughly, and was surprised and a little ashamed at the sudden feeling of anger.

Colour washed into Celia's face and her gaze moved from Will's face and fastened upon a spot in the distant range.

Perhaps she understood things more clearly in this moment than she had done for a long, long time.

Kermody rolled a cigarette and murmured, 'Thanks for all you are doing, Celia,' and was irritatingly conscious of how hollow his words sounded.

But the girl smiled now and nodded her golden head as though understanding perfectly.

'I think I'll go and see Lannigan if Paula's staying here for a while. Maybe I can dress his wound or something.'

'Paula will be here until Thursday night, Celia. That's as long as she can manage – this time.

'I guess Mike would be glad to see you. Reckon he wouldn't mind a sample of some of your cookies!'

Celia nodded. 'I think I'll go now.' She turned enquiringly to the foreman. 'Everyone's over to Cedar Creek, except Chuck–'

'I'll go saddle you a horse,' Will said and turned in the direction of the corrals. 'Come to think of it, Celia, if the men are working the Cedar Creek section I'll ride along with you when I've had a word with Ward.'

The girl nodded. 'And I'll change into something more suitable than this dress. I brought some riding clothes with me.'

The buckskin and Dewey Ruskin's paint Will led into the corrals, replenishing the water-trough and forking hay.

Then he walked back towards the house, leading two fresh horses, saddled and bridled. There were no side-saddles at Stirrup – Paula had always ridden astride – so Celia would have to do the same.

He tied the ponies at the rack and went into the house, taking the stairs three at a time and reaching Ward's room.

He knocked and entered quietly and found father and daughter laughing and crying at the same time.

'Thanks for bringing her, Will. Paula's told me how you braced Ben. It makes me feel like taking a shot-gun to him, even though he is Paula's husband.'

'I've been near to shooting him once or twice myself, Ward,' Will said quietly, 'but a rope might do the trick,' he finished enigmatically.

'Hey!' Ward shouted. 'Where's my nurse? I'm plumb out of water.'

'Celia's going over to see Mike soon. You're not the only wounded son-of-a-gun around here. I didn't mention it before, but Mike stopped a slug. Nothing much, just a scratch,' Kermody grinned. 'I reckon now Paula's here *that* news won't hurt you!'

'I'm sorry about Mike. Come to think of it, I heard Sid Vincent mention Fred Robards. I didn't think to ask him where Mike was.'

'It doesn't matter, Ward. Mike'll be up riding before the week's out.

'Paula! You'd best come down so we can

drink our coffee. I think I hear Chuck moving around on the gallery.'

The girl nodded and rose from the bedside chair.

'I won't be far away if you want me, Dad,' she smiled.

Will turned at the door. 'I'm going out to Cedar Creek to see how the count's going–'

Ward nodded. 'Celia can ride with you, huh?'

Out on the gallery, Chuck was hovering with coffee-pot and cups and a moment later Celia joined them.

They quickly drank the steaming coffee and then Will and Celia Owen climbed into saddles and set out for Cedar Creek.

Paula watched from the veranda, a strange, unfathomable expression in her eyes.

Laura Paramour stood at the roulette table, spinning the wheel for the last of the tired players.

It was fortunate that at this very late – or rather early – hour, most of Clear Fork were making for truckle-beds and tar-paper shacks. Fortunate, because Laura's mind, or a good half of it, was wrestling with her own personal problems.

For the hundredth time, it seemed, she again went over the scene in retrospect when Paula and Ben had appeared and Ben had asked her to share Paula's turn at the roulette wheel with Belle.

Mrs. Mackinnon, Ben had announced suavely enough, for all the liquor he was carrying, was going to visit her father at Stirrup and would not be back until Friday.

The unexpectedness of such an announcement, the first ever of its kind since Ben and his wife had come to Clear Fork, had robbed Laura of her usual ready wits.

Never before had Ben allowed Paula to leave the mining camp except with himself or some suitably trustworthy henchmen, and suddenly Laura realized here was a heaven-sent opportunity for her to get the news to Will Kermody about the forthcoming attempt by Ben's men to seize a good-sized herd of Stirrup beef.

Again, it had been unfortunate that Laura had herself just missed seeing Will on this, his second visit, and nothing in the ensuing conversation gave any indication that he was waiting right now in the livery.

True, if Laura had thought about it, she could have guessed as much. It would be a safe bet that Kermody would escort Paula on horseback and not attempt to employ the slower and trickier alternative of taking a buggy or spring-wagon. It would have been feasible, Laura realized, except that neither Paula nor Kermody would consider a means of transport such as that, when horses were available.

Even so, there had been no time, not one second, when Ben had left them alone together.

He had followed Paula into her room whilst she changed and had even, affably enough in his surprising and new-found consideration, carried the blanket roll downstairs, alternatively talking to his wife and giving Laura instructions interspersed with loosely worded talk about 'compensation'.

Laura's lip curled at the thought. Ben Mackinnon's idea of compensation for day and night work might not be quite the same as Laura's!

And Mackinnon had even seen Paula to the door and watched her cross the street, and had turned back to Laura, as though all along he had divined, somehow, her burning desire to speak to Paula privately for a few moments.

Now Paula had lit out, presumably with Kermody, and sometime before the week was out, Laura knew, this raid was planned and Ben would cash in on stolen Stirrup beef.

It was not too late, yet, of course, to warn Will. It was rather a question of the means at her disposal, and Laura had little enough opportunities herself to undertake a long, arduous journey and back. Especially now, with Paula's work to be divided between herself and Belle.

She tiredly reapplied herself to the task of spinning the wheel, and after a few small wins by one of the remaining players, luck changed for the house and disgruntled players threw in as Laura raked chips and money across the baize-covered table.

She felt all in. She just couldn't have coped with an over-amorous drunk tonight, she told herself as she handed the money over to Lacy, Ben's house-gambler, for locking up in Mackinnon's safe.

With a start of surprise Laura realized the huge room was empty, and exhaustedly she sank into one of the chairs and leaned her bare arms on the beer-stained glass-littered table-top.

The swamper was nowhere to be seen, so that Laura scarcely bothered to look up as Ray Clarke began the chore of wiping tables and washing those glasses which still remained where men had sat and played.

She was surprised, however, when Clarke's massive hand stretched out holding a shot glass of whisky.

'Drink that, Laura!' he growled. 'You look plum tuckered out.'

It was not often that Laura Paramour let down her defences to the world and demonstrated that the exterior hardness did not extend right through to rock bottom.

But tonight she seemed powerless to fight back against things and felt too worn to continue the masquerade.

Ray Clarke saw her for what she was. Outwardly a gilded lily; inwardly an unhappy woman.

'Cigarette?'

Laura jerked up her head and found the barman offering her a hastily rolled quirly. It was Clarke's second act of kindness within the space of seconds, and rather than hurt his feelings Laura would have smoked a hundred corn-paper cigarettes straight off.

As it was, she felt the tobacco's soothing influence almost at once. The unaccustomed rye, instead of making her light-headed, seemed to have cleared the cobwebs from the recesses of her weary mind.

She studied Clark with a newly born interest.

'That did me good, Ray,' she said presently. 'I think I'd like another drink.'

He nodded and went back for the bottle, returning to the table, and meticulously poured the liquor into the two shot glasses.

'Will Kermody's paid for these and then some,' he grinned, 'so I guess we's entitled to 'em.'

'You like Kermody, Ray?'

Clarke considered the question, holding his bearded chin in the heel of his left hand.

160

He grinned suddenly.

'You know, it's kinda funny, Laura, but before that jasper hit Clear Fork I didn't much care what happened to folks – any folks – you, me, Miz Mackinnon. Now, well, it's like Kermody's made me see things more clearly somehow. I dunno quite how to explain. I guess it sounds kinda loco to you, Laura. I reckon I felt like a louse after I'd cooled down a bit and after Will Kermody had knocked Art Millar's front teeth through to the back of his neck! I reckon I enjoyed that!'

'Supposing it happened again, Ray? What then?'

The barkeep's face darkened. 'If Millar lays his hands on you again or any other drunken bum, then I guess I'm goin' to try out my shot-gun, Laura. Reckon that goes for Belle too, or any of the others. That is ef'n they don't *want* to be pawed!'

Laura's heart beat a trifle faster. She was sure now that Mackinnon had left for the ranch and had given Lacey the keys and instructions to close up for the night.

'Don't you ever have a day off, Ray?' she said wonderingly. 'You always seem to be around. I guess, like you, I ain't thought much on these things before.'

Clarke grinned. 'That's funny, Laura, you sayin' that, because Gil Westmacott the swamper's off today an' tomorrow he's takin' my place an' *I'm* off for the day. Fust in a month. Christ knows why I stick this joint!'

'You want something to do?' Laura asked eagerly, then, recollecting what any man like Clarke would do on his day off in Clear Fork, her face dropped.

'What you want?' Clarke demanded.

'It doesn't matter,' the girl said. 'I guess I wasn't thinking. I was only figuring that if you were going to be at a loose end...' She laughed a trifle hysterically. *Maybe the liquor's hitting me at that*, she thought.

Clarke was also thinking of the red-light district in town, but he was unaware that Laura had thought of it first, in connection with himself.

The barkeep was silent for a few minutes as he struggled with himself. He rolled and lit a cigarette and gave himself another drink.

God! She's beautiful, he thought, and jerked his head up with a sudden decision. 'What's on your mind, babe?'

She hesitated for a moment and then plunged recklessly into her idea. She was still uncertain how much Ray was *for* Ben Mackinnon, or how much he would side her and Kermody *against* the boss.

There was only one sure way to find out whether the iron was hot and that was to grab it!

162

'Listen, Ray,' she said eagerly. 'I overheard Selby Lynn and a man called Brad somethin' planning to buy stolen beef off Ben.

'They were in the next room to mine and I couldn't help overhearing what they said!'

Clarke's sweaty face showed intense interest.

'Go on, Laura!'

Encouraged, the girl plunged on. 'Ben's going to send out a crew of night-riders as far as I can make out and lift about a hundred head of Stirrup beef, sometime between now and Saturday.

'Selby figgered Stirrup's got so many steers that Ben's riders'll be able to cut them out without too much trouble.'

'How d'ya know it's got to be afore Saturday?' Clarke asked.

Laura moved her hands sharply in a gesture almost of impatience.

'I heard someone say, maybe it was Kermody himself, that they were on round-up and were cutting out a trail-herd to be on the move by Saturday!

'The point is, Ray, I didn't get a chance to talk to Paula about it. Ben's been here most of the time since then. Only once was he out and then I couldn't find Paula.

'Now she's gone to see her father, Ward Cabot. She could have warned Will if I'd only been able to tell her.'

Sudden comprehension flickered in the

barkeep's eyes. 'You want *me* to warn Will Kermody? Is that it?'

She nodded, unable now to trust herself to say more.

'It's a dangerous game you're playin', Laura,' Clarke said slowly.

The girl bit her red lips. 'Does that mean you don't want any part of it, Ray?'

Slowly the big man moved from side to side. Clarke grinned. 'I didn't say that, babe. Though it's some time now since I forked a hoss fer any distance.'

'You mean you will?'

Lights shone in Laura's blue eyes and the golden hair glinted like running gold.

Clarke felt he was inextricably caught up now in this thing. Maybe under other circumstances he would have refused to do it. Maybe he would have been just plumb disinterested. Now, it seemed, things had changed. He owed nothing to Ben Mackinnon, who had treated him no better than a dog. And why? Because Ben knew that Ray Clarke was wanted for *rustling* by the sheriffs of Champion and Davis Counties!

It wasn't a simple matter of quitting a job. If Ray walked out and Mackinnon felt aggrieved, he would put the Law Enforcement Officers on Ray's track. There would be no come-back. Ben was as likely to throw his barkeep to the dogs as he was – well, his own wife. Maybe more so.

'What about mounts?' Ray asked presently.

Laura Paramour leaned forward and placed a soft, white hand on Clarke's hairy fist. She would hardly have been a woman had she refrained from exerting her feminine attraction.

'I can trust Dewey,' she whispered breathlessly, sending her gaze towards the stairs in search of Lacey's return.

'I'll fix for a good horse to be ready saddled in the livery at six tomorrow before the town's astir.

'As for the trading post. You give Zach this–' She reached into her reticule and withdrew a twenty-dollar piece.

'Put it back,' Clarke growled. 'I told you Kermody did more'n pay fer the drinks!

'You figger Zach Keeler'll swap me a hoss?'

'Sure,' Laura said, 'and you can return it and pick up Dewey Ruskin's saddle-horse on the way back!'

'What are we gettin' out of this, Laura?'

The girl shrugged her bare shoulders. She had been wondering that herself. Certainly Kermody would be warned and, therefore, repaid for his opportune intervention when Art Millar had accused her of cheating. Maybe, if they were lucky, Kermody would be able to prepare a trap for Mackinnon's men. But was Will Kermody big enough, or strong enough, to tie a rustling rap on Ben

165

Mackinnon and make it stick?

'I guess all we've got to lose is our lives,' she said with quaint seriousness.

Clarke was thinking, *If Kermody could get Ben Mackinnon, then I could move out when I wanted to!*

CHAPTER 11

RAY CLARKE'S DAY OFF

Will and Celia Owen rode hard, sparing neither the time nor their much-needed breath for small talk. Yet it was after noon when they came up on Cedar Fork and Will guided the girl across the ford and sat watching as she made her way towards the distant Slash M ranch-house atop the long, sweeping slope of wooded country.

Satisfied that the girl was on the right trail and could hardly fail to find her way, Kermody wheeled his horse, recrossing the stream and pointing towards the distant spiral of smoke through the trees and brakes which pin-pointed the position of the Stirrup riders at their work.

In a little under fifteen minutes Will had come upon the scene of shouting men and milling cattle. Dust rose in thick, yellow clouds every time a rider gave chase to another stray or turned back a recalcitrant steer to where the herd was being held in a bunch, preparatory to driving it down nearer home.

Kermody raised his arm as the men spotted him and shouted their welcome. He sat still in the saddle, savouring and enjoying the sharp smell of burning hides; the wood-smoke blown across by the soft wind, carrying with it the faint aromatic smell of freshly boiled coffee.

Presently, Kermody moved over to where Phil Hankins had just ridden in. He watched as the *segundo* stripped rig, blanket and bridle from the sweat-covered horse and turned it over to Tim Furnival, the wrangler.

Hankins stood by the fire, spraddle-legged, wiping sweat and alkali dust from face, neck and hands.

He grinned up at the foreman as Kermody slid from leather and ground-hitched the pony.

Will said: 'You're well up to schedule, Phil, by the looks of things. The boys are doing a swell job.'

Hankins flushed with pleasure. It was rare to receive praise for normal routine work, and when it came from a top-hand like Kermody himself it was all the sweeter.

Now, the *segundo* reached into the tail-gate

of the wagon for another tin mug. He returned to the fire and poured coffee for Will. Tim Furnival was busy in the makeshift corral.

Kermody unbuckled his spurs, hanging them on the saddle-horn, and hunkered down near the fire, sipping the scalding coffee.

Presently he built a cigarette and threw papers and sack across to Hankins. They watched the Stirrup men at work near the branding fire a quarter-mile away.

Kermody broke a long silence.

'Fay Murphy's been into Clear Fork, Phil.'

Hankins's gaze dragged itself away from the groups of sweating men. A startled surprise widened his blue eyes.

'*Fay Murphy*, Will? Are you sure? But he's–'

Will said thinly: 'Sure, he's supposed to be at the eastern line-cabin with Jim Stewart, but his horse had been put up at Zach Keeler's. I saw it there myself and Zach said he had taken another mount and headed for Clear Fork.

'There may be a perfectly innocent explanation, but I doubt it. If he or Jim were in any sort of trouble they would have made for the ranch – not ridden to Clear Fork!'

'What you figure, Will?'

Kermody drew thoughtfully on his cigarette. 'Both those hombres have had a chip on their shoulders for some time, Phil. It could be some kind of a double-cross–'

'Maybe Fay's got a woman in Clear Fork?'

'Maybe,' Will agreed, 'but one thing's certain. He no longer puts Stirrup first, and that's no good, Phil.

'I guess that goes for Stewart, too, since presumably, if he was not working in with Fay he would have ridden in and told us what was happening.'

'You figger they're plannin' something, Will?'

Kermody considered this. 'I'm not sure. But it means that they've got to be watched carefully, and we've none too many hands as it is, particularly with the trail-drive coming off for Saturday.'

'You're plannin' to trail-drive, whatever?'

Will nodded. 'I'm not sure yet whether the both of us ought to go to Brand City.' He paused and then went on to tell Hankins everything concerning his trip to Clear Fork and his suspicions concerning the rustling of Stirrup and Slash M beef.

'Maybe Murphy and Stewart have had a hand in it then,' Hankins suggested.

'They could be working for someone in Clear Fork. Someone like Ben, for instance. But at the moment we're just guessing.

'I mentioned kind of casually in Clear Fork that we were trail-driving at the week-end. Maybe that will produce some results!'

Phil Hankins nodded. 'We'll have to pull Stewart and Murphy off the cabin by Friday night latest so we're ready to start by dawn on Saturday.'

'You do that,' Kermody said, 'and watch those pilgrims. Reckon you might give them a long spell with the drag-herd,' he grinned. 'You'll have Bred, Sid, Tim and Birdie for point and flank riders. I reckon maybe I'd best stay behind. I've got a hunch this rustling business is going to develop some very soon.'

Phil Hankins's hard gaze lifted to Kermody's face. 'Ef'n you can pin anythin' on Ben Mackinnon, Will, I'll sure be pleased. I figger somehow Paula's not too happy in Clear Fork—'

Again Will nodded. 'We used to have some good times with that tomboy before she upped and married Ben,' he said, now coming to his feet. He looked out across the range, for once with eyes that did not see.

'He's treating her bad all right, Phil. Make no mistake about that. He's going to swing for this cow-butchering *whether he's guilty or not*!'

Hankins felt a cold shiver travel down his spine in spite of the sweat on his body. He had just looked into Will Kermody's eyes.

It had been around 3 a.m. when Ray Clarke had eventually tumbled into bed, yet that part of his subconscious mind on which he relied in lieu of an alarum did not fail him this morning with its gently urgent stirrings.

He sat up slowly on the cot and knuckled the dregs of sleep from his eyes, and thought of the chore ahead.

He figured it was a hell of a way to spend a day off. To rise before dawn after a bare two hours' sleep; to ride like a Pony Express mail carrier all day with little rest and to return at night, all being well, ready to start another series of sixteen-seventeen hour days!

He passed a hand over his bearded face and swung his reluctant body out of bed.

At the washstand he poured cold water from a cracked pitcher into a tin bowl and sluiced face, hands and arms until he was thoroughly awakened. He dried himself on a comparatively clean towel and then donned denims and a calico shirt.

Next, he pulled on a pair of scuffed half-boots and finally shrugged into an ancient fustian jacket. He tied a red kerchief around his neck and found a battered black stetson in his box.

As an afterthought, he reached down further into the box and withdrew a long-barrelled six-gun. He eased back the hammer and spun the cylinder and found that each chamber was loaded.

With a grunt, he shoved the gun into his

waistband, buttoning the loose coat so that the gun did not show.

He made his way past Lacey's and Laura Paramour's rooms and the one shared by Belle and several of the girls, knowing that they would all be sleeping like logs until roused by the swamper.

Downstairs, in the back kitchen, Ray found a plate of cold steaks and a pitcher of milk. He grinned to himself as he drank and hungrily tore at the meat.

He found a box of crackers and stuffed a handful of them in his pocket and then, on a sudden impulse, crossed through into the bar and removed a pint bottle of rye from one of the glass shelves, stuffing the flask into the other pocket of his capacious coat.

He unlocked the front doors and let himself out, openly enough, and laid his glance along the all-but deserted street. It was barely daylight, but he identified Gil Westmacott, the swamper coming towards the Golden Dollar to commence work after his day off.

Ray didn't want to semaphore his movements particularly, so he quickly turned from the board-walk so that a jutting building cut him off from Gil Westmacott's chance gaze. When he heard the swamper go inside the saloon, Ray angled across the street down towards the livery.

Dewey Ruskin was fast asleep in his office,

172

but the livery doors stood open and a saddled horse was standing just inside, its reins tied to a post.

Clarke grinned. Laura had done her stuff and Dewey had come here extra early to cut out and saddle the horse, but Dewey could see no point in going without that extra hour's sleep, so he had promptly retired to his office to make good his broken rest.

Quietly, Ray climbed into leather and urged the steel-dust out on to the street. The horse, scenting the early air and ripe for exercise, took some holding at first. But once clear of the settlement, Clarke gave it its head, finding difficulty at first in co-ordinating the rise and fall of his own body with the fast, bumping movement of the racing animal.

But it came back before long. A man who has ridden in the past cannot forget, any more than a swimmer can. It is strange at first and then suddenly and almost un-noticed it returns. Thus it was with Ray Clarke, and before the sun had lifted above the distant Spanish Peaks, he was beginning to enjoy himself hugely.

After the steel-dust had dissipated its first wild exuberance, Ray pulled the animal to an easy, mile-eating lope and wondered again why he was voluntarily engaged on this dangerous chore.

A vision of Laura Paramour's face flashed

before his mind, as it had appeared last night, or rather early this morning, the hair gleaming gold, the full, red lips parted as she put forward her idea and the blue, sparkling eyes that warmed as they searched his face.

Was it so much because of wrenching free of Ben's grip that he was doing this thing, or was it more because of a golden-haired girl who–

Clarke's train of thought was sharply interrupted by another. Did Laura think anything of him as a man, or was she just using him as the only available person to do such a chore?

Maybe, Ray grinned, tugging at his full, black beard with one hand, *she figures I look more like a hairy ape!* He was reminded of talk he had overheard in the red-light district amongst some of the cheap, painted women, and memory of hours spent in the arms such as these brought a sudden and unexpected feeling of revulsion. For once in his life, the uninhibited extrovert was dissatisfied with himself. He had looked inwards, deeply, for a change, and was mildly shocked at what he saw.

He cursed loudly at his thoughts, and pulled the steel-dust to a halt to give both rider and beast a blow.

He rolled a cigarette and lit it, blunderingly searching his mind and heart for these excitingly new will-o'-the-wisp thoughts and feelings, rather like a mountain bear threading a way through a room of porcelain and china-ware.

An almost childlike idea came to him then, and he grinned with simple pleasure. He would shave off his beard, comb his hair and smarten himself up a bit, before he saw Laura again. It would be interesting to watch her face!

Ray Clarke grinned again and drew on the last of his cigarette, crushing it out between his tree-stump fingers and hurling it away.

He shook up the pony and rode hard enough to reach Zach Keeler's place by a little after 10 a.m.

Keeler came out as he heard the clatter of hoofs in the yard and surprise showed in his bright eyes as he identified the figure of the barkeep astride one of Dewey Ruskin's livery mounts.

'You takin' up a riding job, Ray?' Keeler grinned, leading the lathered beast around to the corrals.

'Naw,' Clarke grunted. 'Figgered I'd ride to Stirrup and back on my day off. Haven't done any ridin' in months. Gawd, I'm plumb sore already!'

Zach unsaddled the sweating horse and turned it into open pasture. He lumbered back to the yard where Clarke was waiting.

'Want somethin' t'eat, Ray?' Keeler said.

Clarke nodded and reached down to the saddle which had been dumped on the ground and withdrew the whisky bottle. 'And some cawfee, Zach, with a drop o' this to help it down!'

A half hour later Clarke pushed back his empty plate and stirred his third cup of coffee laced with whisky.

'So Miz Mackinnon an' Kermody rested up hyar till early this mawnin', Zach?'

Keeler nodded. 'You won't overtake them. They'll be at Stirrup by now–'

'I got all day,' Clarke grinned, 'and I'm enjoying myself for the first time in months even if I have got a sore seat!'

'Today's Wednesday,' Mackinnon said, puffing at the long, black cigar held clenched between his big, white teeth.

'Tonight, Art, I want you and Nick to make a scout and find out exactly where they're holding the trail herd.

'Study the lay-out carefully, so that when Thursday night comes you'll know just what you're doing, even if it's cloudy or raining.' Ben paused and fixed the diminutive Nick Flore with a steady gaze.

'You got those other riders, Nick?'

The gunman nodded. 'Frank Settle, Wick Tolliver an' Bill Eastman. They know what's expected of 'em an' they know what happens ef'n they lose their haids!'

176

'Good! And you'll have Slim and Lee to side you as well. Art will be in charge.'

Nick Flore's black gaze slid quickly over Millar's face, but he only grunted in reply to Mackinnon's instructions.

'What we do if we run into Stirrup riders, Ben?' Art Millar said presently.

'If you run into riders on your scout, Art, then we'll probably have to call the raid off altogether. It's up to you and Nick to see that you don't run into *anything* tonight.

'Tomorrow may be different, though I'm still hoping you men have got the brains and the ability to cut out a hundred beeves without stirring up Pilgrim Valley!'

'We'll do et, boss,' Nick said confidently and Art Millar nodded his big head.

'We'll play this safe, Ben. I'll get around to Kermody in my own time!'

By the time the Stirrup buildings came in sight, Ray Clarke was so sore and stiff that he hardly knew how to stay in leather.

The first bright sparkle of novelty had worn thin, as thin as the seat of his pants, Ray thought sardonically. If he could have his choice again, it would be to say 'no'; to stay in bed until late and then eat and drink and later saunter down-town and seek forgetfulness in the arms of one of Flo Pelisser's girls.

His mood was low and he knew it. Laura's

shining face was no longer clear in his mind's eye and the noble resolve he had felt when she had sat close to him at the table in the bar was now no more than a vague memory.

He reached into the saddle-bag and finished the last drop of whisky, spilling some as Zach's sorrel, scenting water and rest ahead, broke into a sudden canter.

Clarke cursed and decided that there was no pay-off in considering what might have been.

He had thrown in his lot with Laura in this thing and would see it through, as much for her sake as Kermody's.

Nevertheless, Ray, for all his brute strength and obvious toughness, felt the sweat at the back of his neck go cold as his imagination began to paint a picture of Ben Mackinnon's wrath if Ben should ever find out about this!

He pulled up at the rack in the yard and slid from the hull, standing perfectly still, trying to control the shaking in his legs and forcing flogged muscles to respond to his tired brain.

Paula, hearing a rider, had come to the veranda. When she saw Clarke swaying there like a punch-drunk prize-fighter, she called sharply and urgently to him, running down the steps and hurrying to the rack.

'What is it, Ray? What's the matter?'

His glazed and red-rimmed eyes stared at

her for a moment without recognition. Then slowly he grinned and wiped his sweat- and dust-covered face and neck with his neckerchief.

'Gimme a drink, Miz Mackinnon,' he gritted. 'I ain't ridden like this in years–'

'*What is it, Ray?*' Paula insisted.

'Nothin' that won't keep a few minutes,' Clarke said, lurching towards the veranda and ascending the steps like a tired old man.

Paula followed and without wasting further words disappeared inside the house.

In a few moments she was back with a bottle of whisky and a glass.

She sloshed a quarter pint of raw liquor into the glass and set it on the table where Ray had sunk exhaustedly into a rocker.

He drank gratefully, feeling the sharp, raw spirit cauterize the dust and dirt of the trail from his dry throat.

Presently he put the glass down, wiping his mouth and beard.

'I came to see Kermody, Miz Mackinnon. Is he around?'

Paula shook her head. 'No, Ray. He's out branding and getting a trail-herd ready...'

Ray nodded, deciding, in his full knowledge of the situation between Ben Mackinnon and his wife, that Paula could be trusted with this thing.

'Ben's figgerin' on raidin' Stirrup an' cuttin' out a hundred head from thet trail-herd. Laura done told me only early this mawnin'. She overheard Selby Lynn an' Brad Killigrew talkin' in the next room. Ben's riders are to cut out the beeves an' drive them over to Clear Fork to – well, I figure to Killigrew's and Lynn's ranches.'

'What then, Ray?' Paula whispered.

Ray shrugged. 'Reckon its butchered stuff they's after, Miz Mackinnon, to feed the settlement, so I guess the steers'll be killed an' the brands blotted, or else cut out an' sold mebbe–'

'When is this to be, Ray?'

Clarke stretched out for the glass and finished his drink before replying.

'That we don't know, except that it'll be before Saturday. That leaves tonight, Thursday or Friday. You can take your pick!'

'You came to tell Will about this, Ray? Why?'

Clarke considered this as he rolled a cigarette. He was beginning to feel better. His legs were not so shaky now and the whisky had stiffened him somewhat.

'Kermody's an all-right hombre, Miz Mackinnon, fer one thing. Secondly he did Laura a favour when he pasted Art Millar. Laura was kinda grateful for that. So she figgers to even things up by lettin' Kermody know what she heard, so he can be prepared–'

Paula nodded slowly. 'I see. But aren't you

180

taking a big risk in being the one to bring this news, Ray? Suppose Ben should find out someone's talked? Suppose he puts his finger on you?'

Clarke grinned. 'I been tryin' not to think o' that too much,' he said. 'I reckon I'm a sucker when it comes to–'

Sudden understanding lit Paula's blue-grey eyes. 'You love her, Ray?'

The barkeep shifted uneasily in the chair. For perhaps the first time in his life he felt embarrassed.

Paula sat down now in an upright chair near the table.

'Thank you for coming and telling us this, Ray,' she said quietly. 'You knew that I would side Stirrup in a matter like this?'

'What else could you do?' Clarke asked in some surprise. 'We all know what Ben's like. Besides, Stirrup belongs to your Pa–'

'I'll get the cook to rustle you some food, Ray,' the girl said. 'Then I'll ride out and find Will. We shall have to be on the watch from now on. I guess Kermody will know how to play this!'

CHAPTER 12

FORE-WARNED IS FORE-ARMED

Paula Mackinnon sat on the chuck-wagon's tongue, gazing at the sea of old, familiar faces.

There was the balding Brec Chase, Dave Swallow (alias Birdie), the rather taciturn Sid Vincent and, perched on the wagon seat, young Tim Furnival. Will was there, too, hunkered down with the rest, his hat pushed back from his dust-caked face, revealing the beginnings of his reddish hair. Quite inconsequently and woman-like, Paula found her gaze returning to Will's sun-blackened face, his level, grey eyes and bleached eyebrows and, in turn, Kermody's glance lifted to the slim, shapely figure atop the wagon tongue.

She had ridden hard to tell them this news and dust powdered her face and clothes, even the darkly shining hair which was now loosely tied with a scarlet ribbon.

Yet trail dust had no power to mask or alter this woman's loveliness and Kermody cursed quietly to himself, even though he kept his face as wooden as an Indian's.

'So now you know, boys,' Paula said, sipping coffee from the tin mug which Furnival had handed her. 'But fore-warned is fore-armed. Where's Phil?' she asked, suddenly realizing that the *segundo* had been absent all this time.

Will stood up and scattered the dregs of his coffee from the mug.

'He's gone to pull off Stewart and Murphy from the eastern line-cabin, Paula. We'll want them down here for the trail drive.'

Paula nodded. 'What are you going to do?'

Kermody said, 'Keep a sharp watch from tonight onwards and if and when they strike, let them cut out their hundred beeves or so!'

Startled glances shuttled back and forth and Kermody smiled grimly. 'Just so's we give them enough rope to hang themselves' – his glance caught the faint shiver that ran through the girl and there and then the ramrod decided that for her own good it would be as well if Paula knew no more than that of their plans.

There were two other men in the group who had not yet spoken. One was Mike Lannigan's hand, Fred Robards. The other was Sam Bassett, 'repping' for Ed Narroway.

Will turned now to these weather-beaten riders.

'This is not your fight, boys, and you've no call to set in–'

Fred Robards' pale blue eyes flashed aggressively. 'Reckon you kin use all the help that's goin', Will, an' I'm settin' in. 'Sides which, we don't know they won't soon be after Circle D or Slash M!'

'Thet goes double,' Bassett drawled. 'Ed would want it thet way!'

Kermody grinned. 'We can use you all right. With Phil and the other two out, we're in for a rough time with our night-guards.

'Has Ray gone back?' Will asked, turning to the girl.

Paula nodded and laughter wrinkles suddenly appeared at the corners of her lovely eyes.

'He didn't know how he was going to make it, though, he was that sore!'

The men grinned and Brec Chase said, 'Reckon thet barkeep deserves a medal!'

'All right, boys,' Will said presently, building a smoke. 'We're ready to move this bunch down towards home. Let's get this camp broken and be on our way.'

The next half hour was one of orderly confusion. Three or four of the hands, with Brecker Chase giving orders, mounted and started getting the cattle on their feet and moving eastwards.

Sam Bassett gave a hand to Furnival with the *remuda* and the chuck-wagon. Blanket rolls were tied and piled into the wagon or else lashed to cantles. Cooking utensils were cleaned and stowed and, lastly, the fires were stamped out.

With the sun lowering behind their back, and gilding the tips of the Goya range, Paula and Will brought up the rear of the cavalcade.

The chuck-wagon driven by Sam Bassett went first. Then came this last few hundred head of cattle with Brec Chase and Sid Vincent point and flank riders and Fred Robards and Birdie at the drag.

Next came Tim, driving the *remuda* in front of him, and lastly the foreman of Stirrup and the owner's daughter.

This way they received a good deal of dust, but neither one cared. They were too used to this life to consider it as an irritation, and Kermody had only to glance at Paula to know that the girl had not been so happy during the past year as she was right at this moment with eyes, nostrils and mouth clogged with thickly stirring dust!

It was nearing midnight when they came to the holding ground, a mile from the ranch, and wearily turned and bedded down the small herd some distance from the main one.

Kermody grinned thinly as he watched the operation concluded in the moonlit night. He was making it as easy as possible for Ben's men to cut out and rustle the beef! Now, instead of Mackinnon's riders having to start in on nearly two thousand cattle, they would be able to select what they wanted from this smaller herd. For Will did not doubt that whoever was in charge of the wide-loopers would carefully inspect the ground first.

Kermody felt that no attempt would be made tonight, though he himself would be with one of the night-guards right through until dawn. For Kermody's intention was to let Ben steal the cattle and haze them back to Clear Fork or whatever destination he had planned. Will would follow and await his opportunity; make sure of pinning this on Ben himself so that there was no possible way for Mackinnon to wriggle out of the net and point the finger at anyone else.

Young Tim had quickly started a fire and was heating beef stew and coffee.

'Is it all right to light a fire, Will?' Furnival had asked. 'S'posin' Mackinnon's riders come tonight and see it?'

'We want them to see it, Tim, and anything else that is normal at round-up time. Mackinnon must know that we've got to move some of this stuff down to home pastures, therefore there's nothing very odd about having a mess-fire going even at this late hour.

'In any case, they know we'll have night-herders out and that the men'll want coffee.'

Tim had nodded his understanding, and

whilst he prepared the meal, Birdie and Sam Bassett had taken first watch at Will's suggestion. After a quick supper, Fred Robards would ride the mile with Paula back to the ranch-house. As they were so close there was no need for her to sleep at the camp and Ward might have need of her...

The moon was quartering over to the west, and Kermody, fighting against the desire to sleep, felt the presence of unseen things.

A few cattle stirred and bawled. Somewhere a coyote gave its half-bark, half-howl. A prairie rat scuttled near enough to Will's horse to make it side-step sharply and out in the darkness a horse nickered and then stopped abruptly.

Kermody could see little except the dim shape of the cattle, and the silhouette of trees along the nearby stream. Over to the other side of the herd, Fred Robards – now returned from the house – was going the rounds, stilling wary steers.

But Will knew quite surely that somewhere off in the darkness, perhaps even with the aid of glasses, bright eyes were watching the scene, studying the situation, and all the time Will was tensed in case this was to be the night of the raid.

But as the minutes ticked by and built themselves into a half hour and then an hour, he slowly relaxed.

The moon was almost away now and the false dawn had already flared and died in the eastern sky.

Will did not allow himself to sleep in the saddle, though he was fairly certain now that Mackinnon's men would not raid tonight. It was too late. Before they could cut out and get their herd well under way they would be overtaken by the dawn of a new day.

It was Thursday now, Will reminded himself, and today Phil would be back with Stewart and Murphy. Those men, Kermody promised, would be given their time just as soon as the herd had been trailed to Brand City and the men had returned.

At this point in his ruminations Will saw the silhouette of Fred Robards show up out of the lightening night.

The men would each take nearly an hour to completely circle the herd, thus they would meet up with each other every half hour or so.

From the nearby camp the soft sounds of movement were blown across to the night-guards as Furnival began his breakfast chores.

Presently, a fire sprang up, died down and blazed again as the wrangler-cook threw on fresh brush and wood.

'Won't be long before we can eat and rest,

Fred,' Will said.

Robards nodded and spat tobacco juice. 'You figger you heard riders earlier on, Will?' the oldster said.

Kermody nodded. 'I'm not so sure about *hearing* them, Fred, but I reckon the cattle sensed them and I had the feeling we were being watched.'

'Reckon I did, too, Will,' Robards grunted. 'Wal, they've had their scout, now they kin start in tonight on their steal.'

'Or tomorrow night,' Kermody said and put his gaze towards the now awakening camp.

'Here come our reliefs, Fred. Let's drift.'

Soon after breakfast Will called the men together to explain what he wanted done in the event of things shaping in a certain fashion.

Phil Hankins had yet to arrive with Jim Stewart and Fay Murphy, but Will decided that the less the latter pair knew, the better it would be for all. He could apprise Phil later of his plans.

'You all heard what Miss Paula had to say,' Will told them presently over a cigarette, 'and either tonight or tomorrow things are going to start happening around here.'

'Ain't you goin' to let us shoot the bustards?' Dave Swallow complained.

Kermody's slight smile ruffled the Indian

brown face for a moment.

'We're going to–' He broke off suddenly as his upswept gaze caught sight of the rider some three or four miles away.

The crew followed the direction of his glance and Sam Basset said, 'Coming either from Circle D or Slash M.'

'Looks like Mike,' Robards grunted presently.

They waited now and as the solitary rider approached, the men, one by one, identified him as Mike Lannigan.

Tim Furnival replaced the coffee pot on the fire and set a clean tin mug close by.

Some ten minutes later a grinning Mike Lannigan rode into the Stirrup camp and slid from leather as Kermody bid him 'light down and eat'.

Mike's arm was still in a sling, but the colour was back in his face and his step was springy and light.

He accepted the proffered cup of coffee and nodded to Kermody's question.

'The scratch hasn't given me no trouble, Will,' he grinned, 'and since Celia Owen's been over, I've had nothin' to do 'cept laze around. She's back at the house now havin' a grand clear-up.'

Will nodded. 'Glad you're here, Mike. We've had news Ben's going to lift some Stirrup beef tonight or tomorrow. Here's what we do. We keep watch tonight as usual and I shall be with the guards all the time. If and when Mackinnon's men move I'm taking out after them to find out, first, where they're being delivered. The idea being that unless we can catch *Ben himself*, red-handed, we won't be able to do much.'

'I'll ride with you, Will,' Lannigan said quietly.

'All right. So Mike and I take out after the stolen beef, keeping well to the rear so they think they will have made a clean job of it. After that, it's anybody's guess what'll happen, but Hankins will have instructions to take the herd as scheduled, starting at dawn Saturday, *whether we're back or not!*'

'Cain't one of us go with you an' Mike, Will?' Brecker Chase said.

Kermody shook his head. 'You boys'll have your hands full with over a thousand long-horns to drive to Brand City. And get this, all of you: Fay Murphy and Jim Stewart will have to be watched. I'm figuring they're trying a double-cross on Stirrup.'

'Then let's brace the bustards an' fix 'em,' Sid Vincent growled.

Will said: 'No! Hankins will give them the drag herd *all the way to Brand City*! That'll take some of the stiffening out of them.'

Dave Swallow grinned. 'I reckon it will. You want for us to act like there's nothin' unusual, Will?'

'You've got it, Birdie. Don't any of you let

on, and take your time from Phil. He'll be here some time today with Murphy and Stewart.

'There's two more things, men,' Will said. 'First I want someone to ride to Selwyn and let Herb Wilson know what's happening and get him to telegraph the Sheriff of Archer County. We may need his co-operation later when it comes to making a case out against Ben.'

'I'll ride to town, Will,' Sid Vincent volunteered. 'What else?'

'We've got to get all this settled today,' Kermody said, 'in case Mike and I are gone by tonight. I'd like someone to ride back with Paula, Thursday night. Whoever goes can save himself a long ride back by returning on the stage.'

Fred Robards spat and swivelled his gaze round to Kermody's face.

'I kin do that chore, Will, 'specially as I ain't ridin' with the trail crew Saturday.'

Will nodded. 'That's fine, except that Celia will be left up at Slash M alone.'

Mike shook his head. 'No, Will. She figgered on returnin' to Stirrup this afternoon, anyway. It won't make no difference.'

Celia Owen walked slowly from room to room of the Slash M ranch-house, clutching a mop and broom in one hand and a pail of water in the other.

In her eyes there was a bright gleam that boded no good for spiders hiding in dark corners, carefully camouflaged with cob-webs.

She had started upstairs, making her way with a kind of implacable enthusiasm. Every wall being dusted, every floor being swept and scrubbed. Now that Mike was out of the way she could get along like a house on fire, but, woman-like, she sat back on her heels for a moment and thought about the blocky, 'uncouth' owner of Slash M. She wondered why she had ever identified Mike with that particular adjective. Maybe he had not had an eastern education, but *uncouth*? Landsakes! A girl had only look to see the solid gold underneath that craggy exterior!

She sighed rather wistfully and re-applied herself to the task of cleaning.

Pests and vermin of all kinds were routed out of dark corners and driven further afield. The boards began to glisten with the scrubbing they had received and now Celia made her way downstairs to the kitchen and big living-room, setting herself the task of cleaning and putting everything ship-shape.

Quite by chance she discovered a bolt of gingham and with sudden inspiration glanced at the burlap-covered windows.

She opened her reticule and withdrew needle, cotton and scissors, and for the next few hours she was absorbed in the work of running-up curtains for all the downstairs windows.

If the material allowed for it, she would do the same upstairs, she told herself with a small smile, but first she wanted to complete the ground floor.

Living-room, kitchen and hall windows now had their quota of gay, red-checked gingham curtains.

Sunlight gleamed through the fresh, stiff material, giving an added aliveness and brightness to the ranch that had been dismally absent before.

She paused long enough in her task to boil coffee in the kitchen and peck at some food she found in the cupboard. Then, once again, she set to work, her needle flying through the material as she hemmed with a skill and care born of long practice.

Mike won't recognize the place, she told herself with a smile, as she put down the completed upstairs' curtains and went in search of more string and hooks from which to hang them.

It was late afternoon before she had finished, and tired but strangely pleased, she walked out into the warm evening air, surveying her work from the veranda and then turning to gaze out across the range.

Her thoughts travelled now to Selwyn and her dress-shop. She wondered whether there had been any orders during her absence, and smiled at the very thought. There was scarcely enough work to keep her going and sooner or later she would have to face up to the future. What would she do? Perhaps Mike would ask her...? She considered this angle now, exploring the possible consequences, and finding them not so unpleasant. There was a haven here, she felt, if she wanted it. She had discovered a new Mike Lannigan during the short time she had been at the Slash M. A man who hid his feelings behind an exterior of almost rough aggressiveness.

She was sure now that Kermody was right. That Mike cared for her, but fearing a rebuff retreated within himself on the occasions when they met.

But here at Slash M he had not had the same opportunity, thrown together as they were, even though for a few brief hours. Sufficient that she had caught his gaze following her about and that, unlike other times, he had not drawn back but had doggedly held his ground. She would not have been a woman had she failed to read the message in his eyes, though his words had been matter-of-fact enough in all conscience.

But still Celia Owen smiled, and turning back once more to gaze at the newly curtained windows, she felt a sudden strange and unusual warmth for this place as though a part of her were already here.

When – if – she came back at any time, it would almost seem like returning home.

She chided herself for such foolish thoughts and swung down the gallery steps and made for the corrals, preparatory to saddling the pony and returning to Stirrup.

CHAPTER 13

RUSTLED BEEF

Marshal Charlie Ridewell sat on the edge of his cot, his long shanks encased in none too clean underwear.

A similarly disreputable under-vest covered the upper part of his rangy frame. The horse doc had only just left and had changed the cumbersome bandage that had swathed his middle for a small plaster now covering the wound on his left side.

The thought that Ridewell had been miraculously lucky in only receiving a rather bloody flesh wound when the gun had gone off was dismissed with almost contempt-uous disinterest.

There was no room in Ridewell's mind, right now, for any contemplation of his lucky escape. His mood was reflected now, black and bitter, in the expression on his lined, saddle-leather face and in the brightly burning eyes.

Somehow or other he was going to make Will Kermody pay for this. But how?

Would it be any good riding to Stirrup and trying to brace the man on his own ground, or would it be better to wait and hope that the ramrod would come back here to Clear Fork?

Ridewell was no physical coward, but there was no relish in the thought that Kermody, on his own ground, would almost surely be surrounded by Stirrup riders.

It remained therefore either to await his chance visit to the settlement or else to induce him to return and so walk into a trap.

The marshal had already considered and immediately rejected the possibility of holding Kermody on some charge.

He knew that even if he were able to clap him in jail – disturbing the peace – assaulting a law officer – attempted murder – he would be unable to make any of these charges stick, particularly as Con McGuire, Sheriff of Archer County, would have to be brought into the picture.

No! There was only one way to deal with that bucko from Pilgrim Valley and that was to shoot him down from cover. Even Ridewell's mind rejected the use of the wording 'shoot him down from ambush'. The finer phrasing satisfied the peculiar workings of his conscience, even though that conscience was well-nigh irrevocably lost in the twisting and tortuous channels of the man's dark mind and soul.

Now the marshal climbed into trousers and shirt, and before pulling on boots and vest, rolled and lit a cigarette.

He thought bitterly, too, of Mackinnon, for Ben should have backed his play and dealt with Kermody in suitable fashion. But according to town gossip, Ben had not only ignored this aspect, but had even let the bustard Kermody ride back to Stirrup with Paula, Ben's own wife!

Ridewell realized now that he could expect no help from Ben. Whatever game Mackinnon was playing, he was holding the cards too dam' close to his chest for any man to copper the bets!

Coming back to Kermody again, Ridewell considered the other and more important reason why Kermody should be liquidated. Quite apart from the pure flame of anger and hatred that Ridewell felt for the ramrod was this other question of stolen beef.

Two men, Cass Newton and Morg Vert, had come to Ridewell with the news that Kermody was carrying a couple of brands cut out of the hides of Slash M and Stirrup beef.

That little transaction engineered by the marshal and executed by Vert and Newton had been both profitable and easy, or so Ridewell had thought.

Only six steers had been taken, two Slash M and four Stirrup, and sold on the hoof to Chick Folsain for twenty dollars apiece, and no questions asked, and apparently the dam' fool Folsain had butchered the beef and left at least two hides some place where they had been discovered!

Ridewell had taken the cash and had given Cass and Morg fifty dollars each. Easy money for an easy chore. Nevertheless, it would seem now that Kermody was on to something. He had come to Clear Fork and information was that he had at least a couple of cut-out pieces of hide in his coat pocket.

Maybe the law wouldn't come into this at all, but if Kermody *did* ever manage to pin this on the marshal, Ben might decide he had no further use for such as he, Ridewell.

After all, Ridewell reflected, being marshal was an easy enough job, and provided he obeyed Mackinnon's occasional instructions, there was always room – and time – to do something else on the side.

Here then, was the crux of the matter, and Kermody, in coming to Clear Fork with those brands, *had signed his own death warrant*!

True, the Slash M man had been with him, but if Kermody could be killed and the brands taken from him, there would be no evidence left of any kind!

Charlie Ridewell grinned coldly as he buckled on his gun-belt and sauntered slowly out onto the board-walk.

Will Kermody tightened the cinch strap on the Stirrup pony and stepped into the saddle.

He lifted an arm in salute to the men at the round-up camp and moved out into the night – across the shadow-painted range towards the small herd which Mike Lannigan was already patrolling.

Kermody had that feeling that tonight was the most likely night, if Ben was going to see this thing through, and a certain eager anticipation constricted the muscles in Will's belly as he put his mind ahead to the immediate future.

It had been agreed that Mike and he should show themselves briefly as distant silhouettes and then to disappear on the other side of the herd. This was to be in the event of riders coming in for the steal and to lull Mackinnon's men into a false state of security. They would expect to glimpse one or two riders at least and might become dangerously suspicious if they were not able to see anyone.

During the day, both Mike and Will had caught up on their sleep and now both men were prepared to night-herd until such time as the rustlers appeared.

Now Will moved towards the vague shape of a rider, recognizing the blocky outline easily.

'Everything set, Will?' Lannigan asked, and Will smiled as he detected even in the tough Slash M man's voice the faintest tremor of suppressed excitement.

'Reckon all we've got to do is wait, Mike,' Kermody said, 'and hope they'll pull it off without any shooting!'

Lannigan nodded. If he and Will were to trail after the stolen beef and the rustlers, in order to find out where the cattle were to be held, or to whom they were being delivered, if they were to do this successfully, they would not want any trigger-happy cattle-thief starting up with his gun. Stirrup would have to show itself then and make a fight of it with no chance of Mackinnon's men pulling out with the beef.

Will glanced at the bedded-down herd, and then up at the sky. Tonight the moon was lately rising behind scudding clouds. On the range, objects were shadowy, indistinct, and the herd, though only a few hundred head, stretched away into the darkness, so that the cattle on the outer fringes were invisible to Kermody and Lannigan.

'I'd best ride a bit, Will,' Mike said presently and Kermody nodded in the darkness.

'Keep your eyes peeled, Mike,' he called softly.

Will built a cigarette and carefully shading the match with his hands and hat-brim, lit it, savouring the sharp sting of the tobacco smoke and wondering again how long they would have to wait.

Maybe an hour, maybe two. He judged the time at about ten o'clock. If Mackinnon was going to raid tonight, the men could not leave it too late for fear of having to haze the steers too far by daylight...

One or two steers raised their heads and stirred restlessly, and suddenly Will's horse nickered. He cut short the sound by reaching forward and clamping his left hand on the pony's muzzle. Unobtrusively he stubbed out the cigarette on his saddle-horn and waited, straining his eyes into the night and gazing out to the western section of the range.

Then, for a moment, Will made out the dim shape of a rider on the edge of the herd. He was sure it was not Mike because the Slash M man had ridden northwards. This man was over to the west in the direct line of Will's gaze.

But it was only for a few seconds and then an extra mass of ragged clouds had hurried to the moon's face, almost dousing the silver-yellow light, and Will could see nothing more than the shapes of the cattle in his immediate vicinity.

He turned his head slightly to the stirring breeze and was rewarded by the distant sound of a horse, and far away, almost inaudible, a man's voice murmured low on the night air.

If he had not been listening and seeking sounds and movement, these slight intangible signs would have gone by unnoticed. As it was, Kermody was keyed up to the highest possible pitch of awareness and he knew with a solid satisfaction that Mackinnon's riders were, at this moment, cutting out a herd of Stirrup beef!

He only hoped that Lannigan would not run into anything...

Not much over a quarter-mile away from where Kermody waited, Art Millar and Nick Flore with their five gun-hands were cutting out their herd.

Gunmen they all were, but they knew how to handle cattle as well.

Nick, Slim Cormal and Lee Tyler started the difficult job of cutting through the main herd and marking out the beasts they would drive.

Some of the cattle were restless enough to have risen to their feet, but Nick Flore and his riders moved slowly amongst them, murmuring and quietening the steers and slowly and gradually chiselling out the selected ones.

Art Millar sat his horse close-by, peering through the uncertain light and watching Ben's men carefully. His would be the responsibility if anything went wrong, because he was in charge. Yet he knew that the fiery little Nick Flore needed even more careful handling than the other gunsels.

But Millar could find no flaw in the work so far. In fact the vague thought that this was all too easy fluttered through his mind and was almost immediately lost as he spurred forward to intercept a dodging steer.

The work went on steadily and quietly. Once Art Millar called a soft warning as his keen gaze intercepted a distant rider. But though the moon and sky momentarily lightened, the Stirrup rider passed out of sight behind the eastern end of the herd.

Nick Flore recommenced his work, his gun-hands taking their time from him and well within the hour they were easing the stolen beef, some hundred-odd head, away from the main herd. In an hour they were well away from the rest, having successfully executed a tricky job under night conditions.

They moved along at a faster pace now,

Nick and Slim riding at point, Lee Tyler and Frank Settle flanking the herd, and Wick Tolliver and Bill Eastman pushing the drag.

Art lagged behind for a while, but seeing no signs of any activity from the rear, soon pushed forward to join the men at the drag.

According to their pre-arranged plan, they turned and moved northwards first, so that both cattle and horses would have to pass over the three-mile-wide strip of shale which for a few miles followed the bend of the Pilgrim River. By taking this route and sacrificing a couple of hours' time they would leave tracks hard enough for any cowpoke to follow. And if the rain came, which it promised to do, such tracks as there were would be obliterated by dawn or soon after.

This way, too, they could use the shallow crossing on Cedar Fork to the north of the more generally used one and at the same time give Slash M a fairly wide berth.

It was Art Millar himself who had known about this shale strip in Pilgrim Valley and it was now serving the rustlers well, or would have done in the ordinary course of events. But behind that stolen beef and the night-crew of gunmen, two horsemen came up at a leisurely pace, knowing where their quarry was and occasionally glimpsing the dark shapes of beasts and riders as they sky-lined themselves before descending into a wash or a tree-fringed draw.

It was more the instinct or impulse of an animal that caused Art Millar to halt suddenly with a brief word of explanation to the men at the drag. Certainly he had no *reason* to doubt but what their back trail was clear. There was the niggling maggot of doubt at work in his brain now, and Art Millar was reminded of his former feeling when the sudden necessity for quick action had driven all other considerations from his mind.

Now he paused, not anxious, but desiring the satisfaction of *knowing* for a certainty that behind them everything was as it should be.

He waited until the now easily moving herd was lost from view and, with a sharp curse at his own uncertainty, wheeled his mount and started back at a slow walk.

He knew the route Ben's men were taking and knew that he could overtake and join up with them any time he wanted to. But first to satisfy himself and dissipate this vague, ephemeral suspicion.

Kermody's horse laid back its ears suddenly and this time Will moved fast enough to muffle the nicker of alarm. Lannigan, too, acted quickly, and followed the ramrod's lead. They were travelling against the slightly increasing wind and therefore Will's horse had scented or sensed something ahead before they themselves, coming up-wind, were detected.

They heard the iron hoofs striking the shale as they both drew to a standstill and out of the dark night a rider suddenly loomed and took shape a bare twenty yards away.

Will and Mike could not be sure that this was one of the rustlers, but Art Millar felt reasonably certain that the two shapes ahead would be Stirrup riders.

He had his six-gun out now and the hammer was back, the metallic click telegraphing its warning to Kermody as he dived for his gun.

It was barely clear of leather before the quiet of the night was shattered by the roar of Art's Colt and the screaming whine of the bullet as it sped past Kermody's shoulder. Now Millar was a bare five yards away, recognizing the man he had been aching to kill since the day Kermody had come to Clear Fork.

He fired again, his second shot coming almost on top of the first and coinciding with Will's own fast-triggered bullet.

But Art's slug had taken the Stirrup horse in the neck even as Will fired, so that the Stirrup ramrod's bullet went wide as he disengaged his boots from the stirrups and landed clear of the falling, thrashing horse.

Lannigan's gun came up and roared and

Millar's shouted curse was still-born as Kermody, on his knees, raised his Colt and fired, grimly watching as the figure of Art Millar jerked in the saddle and then slowly sagged to one side.

Very slowly and quietly Millar's big frame slid from the saddle. Somehow his boots came free of the stirrups and with nothing to hold him he pitched forward suddenly, tumbling to the rocky ground and remaining quite motionless.

In a moment Lannigan had spurred forward and reached for the bridle-reins, but not before Millar's shot-scared mount had threshed its fore-feet in the air and landed with sickening and bone-crushing force on Art Millar's head.

Even in that uncertain light they could see the bloody pulp which had once been a man's face and head.

After a cursory examination Will stepped into the saddle of the dead man's horse.

'Daid!' Lannigan said, and Kermody nodded and then said, 'Wait!'

While Mike held the reins, Will dismounted and off-saddled, uncinching his own rig from the dead Stirrup pony and throwing it onto Art's horse. Saddle, horse and man were left where they were, on the moonlit shale strip. There was nothing that the Stirrup riders could do right now, except move on.

'You figger they will have heard those shots, Will?' Lannigan said.

'Reckon not, Mike. The wind's getting up and it's right in our faces. We'd best push on fast if we don't want to lose them!'

Towards dawn the two Pilgrim Valley men pushed on a little faster and soon, faintly, the soft rumble of fast-moving hoofs came to their ears from the direction of the low ridge hills ahead.

'They're over in that dip all right, Will,' Mike said, and Kermody nodded, understanding the direction in which Ben's men were hazing the cattle.

They were pushing them hard, too, so that by dawn, or soon after, the herd would be somewhere north-east of Clear Fork. Maybe they would continue straight on or else rest up in some quiet place suitable for 'holding'...

Pearl grey and oyster changed slowly, imperceptibly, to saffron and madder and gold in the eastern sky.

In a few minutes the sun would be up in a cobalt-blue sky, the rain clouds having disappeared and the wind having dropped to a hot, oven-like blast.

They munched saddle-rations as they rode, and washed down the dry, cold jerky and crackers with water from their canteens.

Ben Mackinnon's men were driving hard

and fast and wasting no time in making camp.

By the middle of the fore-noon the rustled beef were being driven into a wide basin north of Clear Fork. More of a small valley between the talus slopes of the northern fringe of the Goya range.

Kermody and Mike, making use of every scrap of cover afforded them by the undulating terrain, gradually reduced the intervening space between themselves and the rustlers.

'I'm uneasy about the fact that no one's back-trailed to look for Art Millar, Mike. By the looks of things I'd say he was in charge of this crew. What's the explanation?'

Mike shrugged. 'Thet little gunman bustard thet shot me – what was his name, Nick Flore? – I'd say if he was in that crew he'd push on and be damned to anyone as fell out by the wayside!'

'Maybe so, but it seems strange–'

'Only strange by our methods, Will,' the Slash M owner said. 'We would want to corral any loose riders same as we would a horse or steers if we was drivin' beef. Me, I figure Ben's gun-slicks have bin told to push the beef to a certain place and they's goin' to do it, come hell or high water!'

Will nodded, dismounting and ground-hitching Millar's black horse. He crawled to the top of the ridge ahead and bellied down in the short, spring bunch-grass.

'There's a spread down there, Mike,' he grunted presently, 'and it looks like they're already blotting brands and delivering some of the stuff—'

'If Mackinnon's not about, Will, it's goin' to be kinda difficult to prove anythin', ain't it?'

'I only hope that Herb Wilson and Con Maguire show up when they're needed,' Kermody said thoughtfully.

CHAPTER 14

SELBY LYNN'S PLACE

After Sid Vincent had left the sheriff's office in Selwyn, Herb Wilson sat contemplating the littered desk, his mind mulling over the information which the Stirrup rider had brought.

Slowly he packed his pipe and touched a match to it, swivelling round his chair so that he could gaze out of the top half of the office window, the lower half having been rendered opaque by the simple application of white-wash.

Will Kermody, it seemed, expected Mackinnon's men to raid tonight or tomorrow. It would have to be Thursday or Friday because by Saturday most, if not all, of the rounded-up beef would be on the trail to Brand City, and if any were left behind on the holding ground near the ranch, these, almost certainly, would not be prime three-year-olds.

Vincent had also said that Will thought tonight would be the most likely, as the previous night, Wednesday, he and Fred Robards had almost certainly divined the presence of riders near to the round-up camp and both Kermody and Robards were willing to bet that they had been Mac-kinnon's men scouting out the lay of the land and the disposition of cattle and night-herders.

That being so, Kermody had asked for Herb to get in touch with Con Maguire of Jackson City, Archer County, and request that Maguire meet Herb Wilson at Clear Fork tomorrow as near to sun-down as possible. If this were a false alarm it wouldn't worry Con overmuch, as it was not a great distance to travel, and as far as Herb was concerned, well, it had been his idea in the first place, hadn't it?

He wondered now whether the expected rustlers were really Ben's men or whether Will was going to pin this on him as they had agreed.

Wilson got up and stretched, reached for

his hat and clamped it firmly on the back of his head. It looked as though he would have some riding to do.

Out on the board-walk he paused for a moment, savouring the afternoon air, hot though it was. He noted the hazy line of clouds on the far horizon and made a mental note to pack a slicker.

He tromped his way down the street towards the post-office and pushed his way through the wicket-gate to the inner office.

Sid Erskine, the agent, sat at his instrument tapping out messages and receiving them on his key-board.

He finished what he was doing and looked up and grinned at Wilson. 'Howdy, Herb. What kin I do for you?'

The sheriff found a chair and stretched his legs. 'Give me a pencil and paper, Sid, an' git ready to send a message to Sheriff Con Maguire, Jackson City, Archer County.'

Herb wrote his message laboriously on the crumpled sheet of paper. When it was finished he handed it to the agent, who read it through. It ran:

Can you meet me Clear Fork tomorrow (Thursday) at sundown. Suspect cattle thieves operating in your area.
Signed, Herb Wilson, Sheriff of Selwyn,
Pilgrim Valley, Heath County.

Sid Erskine nodded. 'I'll send it off right away and tell them at the other end to send a rider with the message if Con ain't in town.'

Herb nodded. 'Thanks, Sid,' he said and stepped from the office.

He made his way to Pete Jansen's livery and inside regarded his own sorry-looking beast thoughtfully.

Presently he walked down the runway and put his head round Pete's office door.

'I want a horse that'll keep goin' all day without settin' down an' going to sleep, Pete. My crow-bait ain't good enough for the chore I have in mind.'

Jansen looked up from his paper as he brought his mind round to the business of the livery.

'All right, Herb,' he grunted. 'Thar's a long-legged sorrel in thar, this end. You cain't miss it.'

'Good?' Herb Wilson said.

'It's dam was called Pegasus, Herb,' Pete grunted and his fat face wobbled as he chuckled at his own joke.

Herb regarded him dispassionately for a moment and then returned to the stalls, instantly picking out the sorrel and gauging its qualities.

In a little while he had the animal saddled and bridled. In the saddle pocket he thrust meat and coffee and saw that the canteen was replenished with fresh water. To the cantle he lashed his slicker.

When the horse was ready for the trail, Herb led it out onto the street, stopping at his office for a carbine, which he thrust into the saddle-boot.

He left the sorrel at the rack out front of Pilgrim House and entered the hotel restaurant for a quick meal.

The sun was oven-hot as it dipped behind the southern fringe of the Goya range and Herb Wilson stepped into the saddle and pointed his horse towards the fiery disc in the west. At his back, the line of ragged clouds was slowly moving up from the north-east. He hoped they would pass. There was no savour for an old one, such as he, in riding fifty miles or more at night in the pouring rain.

Kermody and Lannigan lay flat on their bellies, watching the quick brand-blotting by Mackinnon's night crew.

Nick Flore was easily recognizable but the other men were unknown to both Will and Mike.

Kermody knew by the very speed the men were working that the brand-blotting would be a crude, rough-and-ready effort. It would never stand up to a close inspection, particularly as they were having to blot over brands no more than a day or two old.

215

But they were not worrying about this. Speed seemed to be the main essential, and in a surprisingly short time Nick Flore's crew had dealt with two-thirds of the cattle and hazed them out some place beyond the ramshackle ranch.

Will's idea that they had been left to graze nearby was born out by the sudden return of Flore's riders as they dismounted and prepared to tackle the remaining beef.

Once or twice Kermody had glimpsed a big, burly figure emerge from the broken-down ranch-house and talk with Nick Flore and point his arm as though giving instructions and directions.

This would be either Selby Lynn or Brad Killigrew, was Will's sudden thought.

Paula had mentioned those names, given to her by Ray Clarke and, in turn, given to him by Laura Paramour, who had over-heard the conversation between the two men.

Now Will could see the pattern more clearly. Ben's men were delivering the stuff direct and crudely changing the brands. If Stirrup or law men came across these steers before they had been butchered and their hides buried or destroyed, then it would be the buyers themselves who would be in danger of swinging – Selby Lynn and Brad Killigrew – while with any luck Ben Mackinnon and his men would go scot free!

Will began trying to gauge times and distances in his mind and considered that it was almost impossible to dove-tail things as he would have liked.

When Sid Vincent had returned from Selwyn he had told Kermody that Herb was going to bring Con Maguire into the picture, but whether or not the two law men would be able to meet at the time and place suggested, no one as yet knew.

It seemed improbable that Herb would be able to get to Clear Water *before* this afternoon to meet Maguire. Possibly later, and Clear Fork would *have* to be their meeting place.

It was possible that Herb might ride first to Jackson City, but more probably he would arrange to rendezvous with Con Maguire somewhere outside or near to Clear Fork.

It had been difficult to make things more definite than this, Will realized. Nothing much had been known for certain although Ray Clarke had been quite sure about the raid. As it was he and Laura had been right, but Ben could easily have pulled his men off at the last moment, for any reason, or none at all.

Thus, it had not been possible to give Herb any more than a sketchy outline of *probable* events. Now, so far, these events were shaping as anticipated, and as Will watched the branding fires kicked out in the small valley below, and the rest of the cattle rounded up for another drive, his mind began exploring the possibilities as to what action he and Mike could take on the assumption that Con and Herb would probably be around the mining settlement any time around dusk.

Kermody rose to his feet now and Lannigan followed suit. Together they walked back to their tethered ponies.

Will thought, *However we play this, we can't rely on the law stepping in at the crucial moment!*

'What now, Will?' Lannigan asked. 'Follow the second herd?'

Will shook his head. 'Let's go brace that two-bit rancher. We may be able to scare him into something that can be used to put the finger on Ben Mackinnon.'

Mike grinned and climbed into leather and both men put their horses to the ridge and then rode slowly down the gradual slope which levelled off to form the floor of the basin.

When they were a bare hundred yards from the dilapidated buildings a man appeared at the doorway of the shack-like ranch-house. He was a big, loose-limbed man, dirty and unshaven. His thumbs were hooked into his belt and on his right hip was a heavy-looking Colt six-gun.

There was no trace of warmth or friendliness in the man's pale eyes as his glance moved over the two Pilgrim Valley riders. He was trying hard to place these men and felt vaguely irritated at his inability to do so. From where he stood he was unable to read the brands on their mounts.

Without a word, Will dismounted near the water-trough in the littered yard and trailed his pony's reins.

The man watched as Mike rather awkwardly slid from leather on account of his left arm being still in a sling.

Kermody walked forward until he was within a few feet of the man, who had now moved a step forward out from the doorway.

'You Selby Lynn or Brad Killigrew?' Will said.

The man spat without taking his pale eyes away from Will's face. He had long since put this tall, broad rider as the more dangerous of the two.

'What's it to you, mister?' he said after a brief pause.

'Not much,' Will said mildly, 'except you've just taken delivery of fifty-seven head of rustled beef. Rustled from Stirrup by Ben Mackinnon's men.'

A wary light came into the rancher's eyes.

'Who are you?' he demanded truculently; 'and where do you come in on this?'

'I'm the foreman of Stirrup,' Will said

coldly. 'That's where I come in, Selby!' Kermody saw the sudden flicker in the man's eyes and knew that he had guessed correctly, though at a venture, that this was Selby Lynn's place.

'So I am Selby Lynn,' the man admitted, 'and who the hell are you with your accusations of rustling? That's a goddam' serious charge to make, mister!'

'The name's Will Kermody,' the ramrod said, 'and rustling or dealing in stolen beef *is* a goddam' serious charge!'

Suddenly Kermody reached forward, grabbing the man by the shirt and hitting him in the face with terrific force.

Lynn staggered back, crashing against the door jamb and stumbling backwards so that he finished up by sitting on the step.

An ugly look flared in his eyes and temper laid its red stain on the dark, leather-coloured cheeks.

His hand dropped to his gun and the Colt was almost clear before Will's left boot came up and smashed against the knuckles of Selby's gun hand.

Lynn cursed and dropped the Colt, gazing at the torn knuckles from which some of the skin now hung in bloody and tattered strips.

'You're going to spill what you know to the sheriff,' Kermody said thinly. 'You can do it quietly without trouble or you can do it the hard way. How will you have it?'

Lynn rose to his feet slowly, giving himself as much time as possible to think this thing out.

This man Kermody knew all about the cattle in the further meadow. He knew that the brands had been blotted. Lynn cursed quietly and obscenely to himself. Given another two-three days he'd have had that herd butchered, the carcasses sent to willing buyers, north, south, east and west, and the hides suitably disposed of.

'What happens to me if I put the finger on Mackinnon?' Selby Lynn asked, groping desperately for a hole through which to escape.

'I bought them steers even if they are rustled–'

'You paid a low price per head, Lynn, because you knew Mackinnon was sending a crew to steal Stirrup beef. You arranged with him, you and Brad Killigrew, to buy the stuff at fifteen dollars a head provided Ben did the stealing and made good on delivery!'

Selby Lynn moistened his lips with the tip of his tongue. He laid a long, measuring glance on Mike Lannigan, whose hand rested on the butt of his gun, and then his gaze travelled back to the implacable figure of Will Kermody.

Lynn shrugged resignedly and when Kermody said, 'Drop your gun – carefully!'

he complied like any beaten man.

Lannigan relaxed slightly and dropped his hand from the gun-butt, and then, with incredible speed and agility, Selby Lynn spun round and through the open doorway behind him, throwing the door shut with a resounding crash a second later.

Both men outside heard the bolts being shot home.

Will drew his gun and poured lead into the pine door around where he judged the bolts to be. Wood chips splintered out as the slugs embedded themselves, whilst others actually pierced the door.

Lannigan, gun in hand, moved to a window. What glass there had been was mostly smashed and now he reached inside and tore the sacking down, grimly searching for the target on which to line his sights.

It was Will, moving around to the rear of the house, who first the heard the wildly drumming hoofs and moments later glimpsed the crouched figure of Selby Lynn aboard a flying pony headed out across the range.

Will saw now, what had not been apparent before, that the shack-like ranch-house was obviously joined to the outbuildings, barns and corrals by a series of covered-in passageways.

Selby Lynn had, therefore, wasted no time in useless shooting from the house, but had immediately raced through to the rear buildings and saddled a fast mount with incredible speed. Maybe, thought Will, such a man always kept a fresh mount saddled and handy for just such an emergency.

Kermody's rifle was way back in the boot and he lifted the six-gun and remembered that there was only one shell left. He fired at the fast-diminishing figure and although Lynn was just within range, the shot did not unseat the rider or bring the horse down.

By the time Will had reloaded, Selby Lynn had disappeared from view in the distant folds of the range.

Will smiled bleakly as he saw Lannigan hurrying forward.

'He's coppered the bets, Mike,' the ramrod grinned, 'but I think we've got enough to run a bluff on Ben. Selby's not likely to stop until he's well clear of the territory. But Ben won't know that–'

Mike grinned. 'It shore wouldn't be no use our chasin' that horse on these mounts, Will. What's our next port of call, the Golden Dollar?'

Kermody nodded as he neck-reined the almost exhausted black.

The Pilgrim Valley men had not been the only watchers of Nick Flore's crew whilst they had been branding and delivering the rustled steers.

From a point higher up above the basin, and in a more northerly direction, Cass Newton had been watching points, as was his custom.

Often, when following the criss-cross trails that quartered over range and hills, he would stumble across some item of interest; something that he could remark and then pigeonhole in his mind for future reference.

Today he had had a fancy to ride near to Selby Lynn's place, and the odd impulse which had moved him to saddle up and leave his tumbledown shack had proved itself more of a hunch.

It was quite early in the forenoon when he had heard the rumble of hoofs and had glimpsed the stirring cloud of dust from the concealment of the brush thicket.

He had waited and watched, and unlike most men of his kind, Cass Newton could be a very patient hombre.

He had watched with acute interest the scene of activity in the basin below, had clearly understood the picture which was being painted in the brand-changing and the pushing of the main bunch into Selby Lynn's far meadow.

What was more, from his vantage point so high up, Cass Newton had also witnessed the arrival of the two men from Pilgrim Valley. He could recognize them even from that distance by virtue of the fact that he had seen them both in Clear Fork.

At first he had not known their identities, but the news that Will Kermody was carrying cut-out brands of stolen beef had soon trickled through the town, to be examined or rejected according to the mood or interest of those concerned.

Thus Cass Newton and Morg Vert had taken the news to Marshal Ridewell, and thus Cass had confirmed the identity of the men from Pilgrim Valley. Cass Newton believed he saw the picture now complete.

Nick Flore was a Bar 52 gunman and unless he was working the crew on his own account, which seemed highly improbable, he was now turning over stolen beef to Selby Lynn, quite obviously on Ben Mackinnon's instructions.

It looked as though Nick Flore and his crew had stolen Stirrup steers, or at least cattle from Pilgrim Valley, and the two men watching now had somehow caught on to it.

Cass turned all this over in his mind, seeking a way to turn this knowledge to his advantage.

It was no skin off his nose if Mackinnon took Stirrup beef so long as his trails did not cross with those of Cass Newton and Morg Vert and Ridewell. But Charlie Ridewell would like to know that Kermody was as close as this, Cass thought wickedly, and turned suddenly towards his horse, hidden in the brush.

But as suddenly he stopped, deciding to play out the hand. He could never ride into Clear Fork and back in time for Ridewell to intercept Kermody *here*.

But if by any chance the Stirrup man and his side-kick decided to move eastwards...! Cass grinned and sank back on his heels, waiting with the patience of an Indian.

Hours later he saw Nick Flore's crew move out with the remnants of the cattle, and soon after Kermody and Lannigan descended down the western slope of the basin.

What was happening in the yard, Cass could not see, his view now being restricted by the buildings themselves. But presently the sound of gun-fire came up to him loud and sharp.

Less than five minutes later he glimpsed a figure atop a racing pony. It looked like Selby Lynn and Selby Lynn was going to keep riding clear into Montana!

Evidently, Cass reasoned, Kermody had braced Selby Lynn and gun-play had followed. But somehow, Lynn had turned the tables on them at least to the extent of getting away with his life.

Cass thought of those fat, sleek cattle in the meadow waiting to be picked up! If only – he grinned then. As far as Mackinnon and his crew were concerned the thing was over and done with. The only other hombres to worry about, therefore, were Kermody and Lannigan, who were even at this moment mounting their jaded horses and heading out for Clear Fork.

Cass could give them an hour if he liked and still reach the settlement long before they would. His horse was fast and had rested for hours. Furthermore he would take the narrow cut-off to Clear Fork.

Charlie Ridewell would pay for this information, and if the play was rigged properly Ridewell could even things up with Kermody and Lannigan in one go, with a little help from Cass himself.

That would leave a nice bunch of steers for Ridewell to dispose of privately, and if he paid out in the same way as he had done with the four Stirrup and two Slash M steers, then Cass Newton would be pretty well lined for a while!

He grinned again and untied the reins of his restive pony. In a matter of seconds he was riding at a steady lope along the cut-off, already abreast of the two Pilgrim Valley men some few miles south.

CHAPTER 15

CLEAN-SHAVEN BARKEEP

Kermody's horse – the black he had taken from Art Millar in exchange for the shot Stirrup pony – was lame in two feet and badly lathered.

Mike Lannigan's Slash M mount was in not much better shape and the two riders were inexpressibly weary.

Dust covered their clothes and adhered thickly to the sweat on face, neck and arms.

Will Kermody wiped off another fresh layer of dust and heaved a vast sigh of relief as they came in sight of Clear Fork.

It was still light enough to be called late afternoon but dusk was not far away and Will began to look ahead again, wondering whether Herb Wilson was within a mile or twenty of the settlement.

Mike Lannigan spoke his thoughts and in so doing echoed those of the ramrod.

'I'm dreaming of a hot bath and a shave and drink before showing up at the Golden Dollar.'

Kermody nodded and grinned.

'That goes double, Mike. I guess we've

done more riding lately than any Pony Express rider. Ben'll have to keep until we're good and ready!'

'There's a barber shop right at this end of Main, Will. If we can get those crow-baits to the livery we can make that the next call.'

Dewey Ruskin gave the weary punchers an odd look as they turned in their jaded and travel-stained beasts to the livery.

'You look like you've been ridin' fer a week,' he grunted and remembering Kermody's previous generous payment, added suddenly:

'Here, take a pull at this!'

He produced a flask of rye from the pocket of his waist overalls and Kermody smiled and put the bottle to his dry, dust-caked mouth. He poured the equivalent of a couple of shot glasses down his throat and spluttered and coughed. Then he wiped the bottle and passed it to Lannigan.

Dewey Ruskin gazed dolefully at the lowered level of the liquor when the bottle was finally returned, but his face brightened a little as Kermody thrust gold into his hands.

'Barber shop,' Will gasped, still striving to regain his breath, and Ruskin nodded and jerked a thumb over his shoulder.

'Next door,' he grunted, and then, lowering his voice, said, *Watch out for Ridewell and Cass Newton!*'

Both men were outside the livery before the significance of the hostler's whispered warning struck them with a kind of delayed force.

Kermody's wary glance moved over the street, but here, at this end of Main, there were fewer buildings and, therefore, fewer folk about.

'Let's get into the barber's, Will,' Mike suggested.

Fifteen minutes later, in a back room of the clap-board shop, they sank back in the luxury of hot, soapy water in zinc baths.

Aches and pains were driven away by the soothing, steamy heat of the soft water. The fact that in a little while perhaps they might be in a serious shooting duel was something hardly worth considering at this moment.

Presently an assistant came in to turn up the low-burning wicks of the lamps and Will knew that dusk was even now giving way to night.

Reluctantly they stepped from the baths and dried themselves on large, hot towels. When they were fully dressed, Will led the way back to the front room.

Here he gave explicit instructions to the little barber about the placing of chairs, insisting that they be moved against the wall, half facing the door.

The barber objected in his garrulous, fussy way and Kermody began to feel the

slow rise of exasperation. He said softly:
'You can have a gold piece or a leaden pill.
Take your choice and quit yapping!'

The barber looked up at this tall puncher,
saw that he was deadly serious, and immediately went as white as his coat, hastily
swallowing back his next words.

'*Yessir!*' was all he had room for now, and
Will and Mike leaned back in the big chairs
half facing the door.

Under the blue-and-white striped protect-
ing sheet, each man's hand covered the butt
of his gun.

Satisfied now, Kermody allowed himself
to be shaved and to revel in the almost sen-
suous pleasure of wet, steaming-hot towels!

They came out on to the darkened plank-
walk, moving away from the lighted front of
the barber shop and then standing rigidly
still, accustoming their eyes to the darkness
on the street.

They had almost reached the Golden
Dollar when a man's voice, close at hand,
cut through the noise and bustle of evening
traffic.

'*Kermody!*'

Will turned sharply even as his brain
telegraphed Dewey Ruskin's remembered
warning to the nerves and muscles of his
body.

'*Get down, Mike!*' Kermody shouted and
threw himself forward even as the shot

echoed through the street and the bullet passed a bare hand's breadth over his head.

If Will had not fallen forward and downwards, the slug could not have missed burying itself in his upper body.

His gun was out now as he lay half crouched in the dust of Main, seeking his assailant from amongst the men on the walks who were now diving for buildings and alleyways.

Another shot came, this time from the other side of the street, and Will knew the cold certainty of being pinned down by cross-fire.

Mike's gun barked from behind him and still Will's eyes sought the brightly lit buildings and dark shadowed lots on the side of the street.

The walks were deserted now and Will could see more clearly. Perhaps it was because he had, so far, lain quite still. Perhaps it was because his assailant was determined to make sure.

Whatever the reason, Kermody glimpsed the rangy figure of Marshal Ridewell edging its way around the side of the building ahead. No more than twenty paces away.

Kermody drew back the hammer of his gun and waited.

Again there was the crash of six-gun fire and tinkling glass. At least one of the shots had shattered the window of a store or shop.

Will heard Lannigan grunt and heard the Slash M owner's six-gun roar again in a veritable cannonade of shots.

A man screamed from across the other side of the street and in the sudden, breathless anxiety of the moment, Ridewell took a step forward so that his body was lined in Will's sights.

Almost immediately Ridewell sensed the rashness of that move and stepped backwards, but not soon enough!

Kermody's bullet took him in the chest, half spinning him round with the force of the impact. Even then the tough marshal turned slowly, fighting to bring up the gun that was fast becoming too heavy for his weakening grasp.

With a last convulsive effort he squeezed the trigger, but he was almost dead before the bullet had finished ploughing an erratic course in front of Will, ricocheting from a post on to the iron ring of a water barrel and then burying itself in the dirt of Main.

Ridewell crashed to the ground and Mike shouted, 'You all right, Will?'

Kermody nodded and wondered with grim humour whether that were a sufficient answer. He turned his head now and found that Mike was closer than he had thought.

Lannigan grinned, seeing now for himself that Will was not hurt.

'The other jasper's lit out, I figger, Will,'

Mike said, coming forward. 'But you seem to have settled with this one!'

Kermody slowly refilled his gun and sheathed it. He beat dust from his clothes with his stetson and then replaced the hat on his thick, reddish hair.

Men were beginning to appear on the street and along the plank-walks, slowly at first and then more quickly, as confidence was gained. The shooting was over and men crowded round the dead marshal and switched uncertain gazes to Kermody's high figure and Lannigan's square-cut one.

Either by accident or design, Mike's gun was still out, and as before, when Ridewell had been shot with his own gun, no one attempted to brace Will for his shooting of the marshal. They merely looked at him, waiting for an explanation, and Will saw that they were entitled to that, at least.

'We were warned only an hour ago that Ridewell was gunning for us,' Will said. 'Some of you men were watching, you saw the play was rigged. We were shot at from cover and came under cross-fire from Ridewell over there and, I figure, a man called Cass Newton on the other side of the street!'

'Whoever it was,' Lannigan grinned, 'I guess I winged him. He's lit a shuck out. Heard his pony jest after Will got Ridewell.'

'That's right,' one man said, 'I saw two

bursts of gun-fire comin' acrost jest like this puncher says.'

'I heerd the other one's pony, too,' a second man chipped in.

At that moment the doors of the Golden Dollar flew open and a clean-shaven, white-coated bartender came out, a double-barrelled shot-gun in his ham-like hands.

For a second Kermody was nonplussed.

'You all right, Will?' the man asked anxiously and then Kermody grinned.

The bartender was Ray Clarke *and he was clean-shaven with slicked-down hair*!

'Right enough for a drink, Ray,' Will called and both men moved towards the doors as the crowd split and took up once again their interrupted activities.

Mike and Will leaned against the bar and surveyed the big room, filling up for the evening's activities.

Smoke whirled over the heads and shoulders of players and dancers and the low-hanging coal-oil lamps threw down bright yellow light on the lively, colourful scene.

Gil Westmacott was helping Ray at the bar and Clarke was thus able to spare time for a little talk.

Will saw no sign of Paula, but Laura was at the roulette wheel and smiled and waved her shapely arm when she saw the Pilgrim Valley riders.

'You got my message all right, Will?' Clarke said, wiping the bar counter with a cloth and moving the whisky bottle a couple of inches.

'Sure,' Will replied. 'We owe you and Laura both something. Ben's not here yet?'

The barkeep shook his head. 'Don't expect him before about ten.'

He turned to Lannigan. 'You stopped a slug, mister?'

Mike grinned. 'Nick Flore got a mite trigger-happy the other night, but Ben's Chink servant dressed it. Almost healed now.'

Clarke nodded and Will said, still surveying the room: 'There's going to be sparks flying later on, Ray. I'm going to brace Ben when he comes in. One of us won't go out of here alive.'

His voice was so quiet and matter-of-fact that for the space of two or three seconds neither Clarke nor Mike himself absorbed the deadly significance in those softly uttered words.

Clarke said: 'I got the shot-gun handy, Will. If it ends up in a fight, I'm backin' you. I got reasons,' he finished enigmatically.

The barkeep was called away then to help Gil Westmacott with a sudden rush of orders.

Will quietly studied the place through the haze of tobacco smoke. He remarked the faro and monte tables near the further wall and closer the big roulette table where Laura worked the wheel and where, tonight, a houseman was croupier.

There were tables and chairs scattered between the gambling section and the small space used for dancing, most of them occupied by roughly garbed miners drinking and talking.

On the other side of the room was the small stage and Will noticed the coal-oil foot-lamps were alight and judged that there would possibly be a show tonight.

'I'm goin' outside, Will, to keep an eye on things. Mebbe I kin give you warnin' when Ben shows up, or the sheriffs.'

'Don't go starting anything, Mike,' Will said. 'You can't move so fast with that arm in a sling.'

Lannigan nodded, finished his drink and leisured his way to the batwing doors, the picture of a man who has time and money in his pocket to spend freely.

Kermody's gaze returned to the room and swept upwards to the gallery.

He pin-pointed Ben's upstairs room and the further one which was Paula's.

It might be as well, he considered, to warn her about the likely happenings to come. Then he thought again and decided it would be better to let things ride. The less Paula knew about what was going to happen downstairs the better.

A black-coated man moved through the room now, turning some of the lights low as the curtains across the stage were slowly and rather jerkily pulled apart. Four of Belle's girls were standing there, the foot-lights gleaming on their bare shoulders and arms and long-stockinged legs.

The costumes were of the briefest and howls of delight arose from lusty throats and lungs as the miners gave vent to their appreciation.

Will saw now that three musicians were grouped near the piano. A fiddler, a guitarist and a concertina player.

For the next half hour the stage show held the undivided attention of nearly everyone, even the hardened gamblers. Then, the first show of the evening being over, men returned to the games of chance or picked a dance girl to whirl around to the lively strains of the sweating band. Beer and whisky flowed and raucous laughter competed with the general noise and pandemonium.

Will Kermody glanced at the clock and decided that if Ben was not due until at least ten o'clock, there was plenty of time for Mike and himself to catch a meal at the Chink restaurant.

He called to the barkeep and when Clarke leaned over the counter Kermody said:

'We're going to get a meal, Ray. When I come back you nod if Ben's in the downstairs office and shake your head if he's not here. *Sabe*?'

Clarke said: 'And if he's upstairs, Will, I'll wipe the counter with this cloth. Okay?'

Will nodded and strolled out through the batwing doors, thankful that at least he would have Ray Clarke's support if necessary...

'What happened?' Mackinnon rasped as Nick Flore dismounted and handed the reins to Slim Comal. 'Where's Art? Here, come inside and tell me!'

Ben led the way into the big living-room in the Bar 52 ranch-house; the only anxiety he betrayed was in the rather quick and repeated puffs he gave to the cigar in his mouth.

The late sunlight, streaming in through the windows, high-lighted and flared the trail-dust on the little gunman's face and clothes.

Nick removed his hat and wiped sweat and grime from his crinkled, leather face, his black eyes switching to the liquor bottles on the ornate dresser.

Ben crossed over to the drinks and poured a liberal dose of rye into a glass, thrusting it towards Nick's outstretched hand.

Flore gulped down the fiery liquid and

wiped his mouth.

'Smooth as silk, boss,' he grinned. 'Delivered to Lynn and Killigrew safe and sound, as ordered! Here's the *dinero*,' he said, throwing weighted saddle-bags onto the polished table.

Mackinnon unbuckled the bags and glanced quickly at the money, assessing the total amount with the speed of a born mathematician.

'You must have hazed a few over a hundred, Nick?'

Flore nodded. 'I reckon. Maybe hun'erd an' thirty. I jest ferget the tally right now, but they've all bin accounted fer an' paid fer!'

'What's happened to Art?'

Nick Flore shrugged. 'We ain't seen him since we started off, boss–'

'*What*?' Mackinnon roared. 'What in blazes do you mean?'

'Easy, boss,' Nick murmured with a confidence he could not wholly feel.

'Art said he was goin' to back-trail soon after we started pushin' the herd. No one saw or heard us, I'll take my oath on that!'

'Then what?'

Nick Flore shrugged. 'Nuthin' much, I guess. Art was in charge an' he told me to push on with the herd, an' we done jest that. I sent Slim back several times but he didn't see Art nor anyone else.

'Our job was to get the herd outa Pilgrim

Valley, an' by God we did it boss, an' sweated blood changing the brands and deliverin' to Lynn and Killigrew!'

'You didn't kill Art Millar, did you, Nick?' Ben's voice was as soft as the purr of a cat, and for a moment the starch went out of Nick Flore.

He shook his head in vigorous protest. 'No, boss! Neither me, nor any of the others, and Slim and Lee will tell you I never left the point position once!'

'I just wondered, Nick,' Ben said softly, 'knowing that you're kind of impulsive at times. And it does make one less to share the bonuses, doesn't it?'

Flore swallowed hard. 'It does, boss, but none of us had anythin' to do with Art being missin'. We figgered he either run into Stirrup riders or else decided to come back here fer some reason.'

'He's not been back here, Nick,' Mackinnon replied. 'I think we can resign ourselves to the fact that Art Millar won't return either here or to Clear Fork.'

'You mean he's lit out, boss?'

'I mean he's dead, Nick,' Mackinnon said quietly.

Presently Ben rose, threw his dead cigar into the hearth and turned to the gun-thrower.

'All right, Nick. You go and get a meal with the rest of the boys. You'll get paid out tomorrow morning, *sabe*?'

Flore nodded and tromped out of the room.

When he was gone, Ben quickly computed the money in relation to the number of beeves stolen and sold.

There was a little under $2,000; $1,920 to be exact and that meant at $15 a head, the boys had stolen, driven, branded and delivered, one hundred and twenty-eight prime steers. Not bad going for a start, Ben smiled.

Over and above the normal wages he paid, Slim Comal and Lee Tyler would receive an extra $100 each; the three new hands $50 each and Nick an extra $200. Art was out of it now, presumably, so that left a clear profit of $1,370!

There was a good profit in this rustling business, Mackinnon thought, when it was handled properly.

Now, he drew paper and pencil towards him, quickly checking on his mental figures and dividing the money to be paid out into neat packages, each with the recipient's name pencilled on the outside.

He shoved a handful of coins in his trouser pockets and bundled the rest of the money into the big safe against the wall.

He crossed over to the dresser and poured himself a glass of whisky, slowly drinking and silently toasting himself!

CHAPTER 16

SHOWDOWN

They came out of Chen Luing's place and moved with the crowd of jostling miners along the narrow plank-walk back towards the Golden Dollar.

As far as Will could see, there was no sign of any undue excitement on the street and he wondered whether Ben was here and had heard about Ridewell. Whether, having heard, he would do something about it or whether he just didn't care.

Mike stopped suddenly at a darkened alley just near to the Golden Dollar and laid a restraining arm on Kermody.

They turned and saw Herb Wilson leaning against the wall in the half-light.

Next to him was a big man, inclined to fat. His thinning hair was partly revealed by the pushed-pack stetson and his round face was bisected by a pair of blonde moustaches.

His pebbly eyes bored into the two Pilgrim Valley riders.

'Howdy, Herb,' Will said and the sheriff nodded.

'This is Con Maguire, Will. Con, meet

Will Kermody and Mike Lannigan.'

Maguire grunted and tucked the cud of tobacco to one side of his mouth.

'Hear you been busy already tonight, Kermody,' Con said. There was no antagonism in his voice and no friendliness. It was essentially neutral.

'You mean Ridewell?'

'That's who he means, Will,' Herb said.

'He rigged up a nice little cross-fire for Mike and me,' Will said. 'Ridewell was – unlucky. The other one, Cass Newton I'm told, lit out fast!'

'Further he's gone the better,' Maguire said, unbending a little. 'Had my eye on Newton and Ridewell for some time. What you want us to do, Kermody?'

Will said: 'I'm going in there to brace Ben. I'd like you with me, Con, and I'd like Herb and Mike to keep an eye on things outside–'

'Why?'

'We don't want Ben's gun-hands, Nick Flore and the rest, horning in. They're probably resting up at Mackinnon's ranch now, but they might have a fancy for coming to town and spending their bonuses–'

'Herb's given me the picture, Kermody,' Maguire said, heaving himself away from the wall. 'You figure you got proof to nail Mackinnon with?'

Will smiled thinly. 'We'll see. Let's go in!'

The moment Kermody entered through the batwing doors, Clarke looked up and saw him. Will waited a second and then the barkeep nodded his head, very slightly, and turned away.

Kermody felt a cold trickle run down his spine as he moved towards the downstairs office door...

Ben looked up quickly from his desk, and it was evident that he was unpleasantly surprised. Especially when Con Maguire followed Kermody into the room and closed the door behind him.

After the first momentary start, a bland smile chased away the scowl on Ben's face.

'What do you think you're doing, Will?' he asked cheerfully. 'Runnin' an express shuttle service between here and Pilgrim Valley?'

Will's smile was as cold as ice.

'You wondering why Sheriff Maguire's with me, Ben?'

Mackinnon leaned back and pointed to the two vacant chairs.

'Make yourselves comfortable, gentlemen, and we can discuss–'

'This isn't a social visit, Ben,' Kermody said. He stood tall and straight, looking down at the suave, bland face which he had more reason to hate than anything else in the territory. Will's arms hung loosely down at his sides, his right hand a few inches in front of the holstered gun.

'Last night,' Kermody said softly, 'Nick Flore and Art Millar with a few more of your gun-slicks ran off a hundred-odd head of Stirrup beeves. Most of them are on Selby Lynn's spread right now. The rest were hazed over to Brad Killigrew's–'

Ben's smile broadened. 'Go on, Will,' he invited. 'This is a dam' interesting fairy story. I always did think you had a fine imagination!'

Will said: 'The stuff's there all right, Ben, and you know it. Trouble is that Lynn won't have time to butcher the beef and dispose of the hides before I take Con Maguire to see them.'

'Well now,' Ben said pleasantly. 'Like I said, this is all very interesting. Supposing Selby Lynn *has* got rustled Stirrup beef on his spread. How do you know–'

'The brand-blotting was hastily done, Ben. It was merely a precaution. No one figured they would have to be inspected because Lynn reckoned on butchering the stuff and hiding or smuggling the hides.'

'Might I ask how you know all this, Will? Even to the extent of being able to name the – er – rustlers themselves?'

Will nodded. 'Sure! We watched them cut out the beef and followed them all night–'

'We?'

'Lannigan and myself. We trailed behind. I can tell you this, Ben, you won't see Art

Millar again. He's dead and I'm riding his horse–'

'It seems to me you're riding a very *high* horse. What Art Millar does in his spare time–'

'Cut it out, Ben,' Will said tiredly. *'We've got Selby Lynn and he's talked plenty!'*

There was a long silence following these words, all the more pregnant by virtue of the lively uproar sounding through the door to the saloon.

Mackinnon moved slowly, taking the cigar from his mouth and balancing it with meticulous care along the edge of a brass ashtray.

'What did he say?' he asked in a low whisper.

Kermody, watching the man closely, judged the time for action was not yet at hand.

'That Art was in charge with Nick Flore and the rest. That they were acting on your instructions–'

Then Mackinnon moved with such incredible speed that neither Will nor Con Maguire, as tensed as they were, were ready when it came.

In a second, or even less, it seemed, Mackinnon's gun came up and shattered the single oil lamp, plunging the room into total darkness.

Will and Con both moved to the door,

momentarily blinded by the sudden pitch-darkness, and collided with each other.

A few feet away the door opened, letting in light and sound for a brief thought-flash and then slamming shut again.

In one stride Kermody had reached the door, only to find it locked. His gun was out now and gauging the distance and position of the lock as best he could in the darkness, he fired point-blank in rapid succession.

The lock burst, and such was the force of the bullets at close range that the door even sagged open slightly as a result of the shattering impact.

Kermody kicked it open, gun in hand. Beside him, Maguire moved quickly for such a big man. There was a long-barrelled Peacemaker in his right fist, but both men were momentarily blocked by the milling crowd of miners and girls who had started to move the moment Mackinnon had rushed out, locking the door behind him.

Will fought his way through the angry, cursing men and a few screaming percentage girls. He glimpsed Mackinnon at the top of the staircase, making for the gallery.

Will fired and saw the wooden rail throw up splinters of wood a foot from Ben's running figure.

Now Kermody had reached the foot of the stairs and his sudden headlong plunge was sharply checked by the screaming bullet from the exploding gun above.

The slug burned Will's cheek, rocking him back on his heels for a second by the very shock of its nearness. He felt the blood well in his cheek and looked up to see Lacey, the houseman, standing there, pointing the gun.

Kermody pushed Maguire back not a second too soon as Lacey let fly again.

Men and women were charging each other now with a wild, animal-like ferocity born of panic. Anything to get away from those spitting guns and the cross-fire of hot lead.

Another slug clanged onto one of the stoves and ricocheted off, striking the ankle of one of the fleeing percentage girls. Her eldritch scream of pure hysteria rose in a fast upward curve above the noise of shouting, swearing and firing.

A lamp went out and Kermody threw another shot up towards the gallery, taking a chance again as he realized that Lacey was holding them off so that Ben could escape.

There was a sudden scrimmage up there now and Will caught sight of struggling figures only partly visible in the dimly lit gallery.

They came forward, descending the stairs slowly, and Will's gun lifted, but did not fire. He gazed with a kind of shocked horror at the sight of Lacey coming towards him holding Paula in front of his body, his left arm encircling her slim waist.

He was powerful enough to half-carry her as he moved downwards to the saloon, so that the girl's feet scarcely touched the stairs.

Poking out from between her right arm and her body was Lacey's black gun.

'Git back all of you,' he snarled, and Kermody and Maguire retreated obediently. Will's face was bleak and empty as though all feeling had been wrung from him.

Those few miners and percentage girls who had been unable to reach the doors fell back as well, shoving, cursing and tripping over in their fear-laden haste to get away from that gun of Lacey's. Even then he fired just to show the room he meant business and a man went down, clutching his side, mouthing obscenities between shrieks of rage and pain.

Paula's spangled dress had been torn and disarranged during the first moments of her struggle with Lacey, yet she contrived, in spite of this, to maintain a regal air.

Her face was white under the artificial colouring and her eyes turned to Kermody sending out a message almost of supplication.

He lifted the gun at his side, but knew with a cold certainty that the risk was too great.

Lacey was well across the room now and Will saw Ray Clarke watching, helplessly, from the bar. If it were impossible to use a six-gun without danger to Paula, it was certainly hopeless to consider a shot-gun!

Will's glance travelled towards the batwing doors. They were comparatively free of human obstruction. This would be Lacey's most difficult moment and he knew it. What he did not know was that Herb Wilson and Mike Lannigan were outside!

Will thought, *But are they outside waiting, or did they do down in the first mad rush to the street?*

Lacey reached the doors and without warning he released Paula from his grip so suddenly that she half fell to one side, stumbled and caught herself.

The houseman's gun swung once in a wide, menacing arc and Will's narrowed eyes saw a whisper of movement at the doors, then Lacey tilted his gun upwards and shattered the four remaining lamps. Two had already been extinguished in the sharp exchange of shots earlier and now the room was plunged into darkness.

Will moved forward tentatively and Con Maguire's voice close by called softly, 'You there, Kermody?'

'*Hold it everybody*,' a voice rang out, cutting sharply into the clamour of raised voices.

A moment later a match flared and a lantern shone its thin, yellow light into the room from near to the outside doors.

Another lantern appeared and with a surge of relief Will saw Herb Wilson and Mike Lannigan, guns drawn and lanterns in their left hands.

'All right, boys,' Herb Wilson said mildly across the now quietened room. 'Get some of those lamps alight if they're not too smashed up.'

Fortunately it was mainly reflectors and glass that were shattered and only one lamp had been punctured, so that oil dripped in a thin, steady stream. One of Belle's girls gave a high-pitched laugh and then cursed softly as the oil caught her face and bare shoulders.

Kermody had moved across the saloon and in the dim light before the lamps flared again he caught hold of Paula with a wild, urgent grip.

'You all right, Paula?' he said huskily. She smiled and brushed at her eyes with a quick gesture and looked up into the dark, Indian face and nodded.

'I'm all right now, Will,' she whispered. She clutched his arm fiercely as she brought her mind round to bear on the immediate situation.

'Ben's gone to the ranch, Will, to round up his men and get away if he can. He had to get his money from the safe. That's why Lacey played for time and tried to escape into the bargain.'

'I'd forgotten Lacey for the moment,' Will said, looking down at the huddled, black-coated figure on the floor by the door.

Lights were coming awake now and the two law men were re-establishing some semblance of order to the place.

Kermody knelt and examined Lacey. His head was cut and blood oozed from the wound which Will judged had been made by the butt of Herb's or Mike's gun.

'Can you watch this pilgrim, Ray?' Will said, turning to Clarke, who had come round from the bar counter.

'It'll be a pleasure, Will,' the barkeep said grimly. 'I couldn't do nuthin' before.'

Kermody nodded. 'Get Laura to stay with Mrs Mackinnon for a while, Ray. We've got a chore to finish!'

'Ben?' Clarke asked softly. Again Kermody nodded and recrossed the room to join Mike Lannigan and the two sheriffs.

Will and Mike emerged from the livery with fresh mounts.

'How did he get away?' Con Maguire asked as he heaved his vast bulk into leather.

Will caught the reins of his horse and paused. 'Reckon he dropped from the first-story window at back and just came round and grabbed a horse.'

Kermody swung up into the saddle and

Herb Wilson said, 'You and Mike can find Ben's place?'

Will nodded and touched the horse's flanks. Mike came up alongside and, with Con Maguire and Herb Wilson following on close behind, they put their ponies to a fast trot, churning up the dust of Main and turning into the town 'square'.

Once through and onto the trail itself, they urged their mounts to a gallop. Bridles jingled, leather creaked and hoofs pounded the trail until Kermody, in the lead, pulled his horse in, waiting for the others to join up with him.

'There's lights in the bunk-house,' he said pointing to the Bar 52 spread across the meadow.

'Maybe they've not had time to light out yet; Ben can't have been here long.'

'Let's get on,' Con Maguire grunted. 'I guess I wasn't built to be a goddam' jockey!'

They swathed a passage through the bunch-grass, dismounting about a hundred yards from the bunk-house.

Each man drew a carbine from his saddle, after tying his horse to a fence-post.

'We could 'a' done with some deppities,' Maguire growled. 'Still, it's kinda late in the day to think of that. How many you figure there, Kermody?' Maguire had kept his rumbling voice low and now Will followed suit.

'We counted six, including Nick, at Lynn's place, didn't we, Mike?'

Lannigan nodded and Con Maguire turned to the sheriff of Selwyn.

'You agreed on finishing this thing up, without sending for more men, Herb?'

Herb said: 'It's either now or never, Con. If we don't move now they'll most likely be plumb outa the territory by mornin'. May still have gone for all we know, an' left the lights burnin' a purpose.'

As though in answer to this pessimistic suggestion a rifle cracked from the nearby bunk-house and a bullet spanged into the fence-post causing the tied horses to rear and plunge and squeal in terror.

'You get round the back, Herb, and you, too, Lannigan. You kin use a six-gun?'

Mike nodded in the moonlit night.

'Me an' Kermody'll try an' keep this side covered,' Maguire went on. 'Scatter! And mind how you go!'

Another rifle cracked from a different angle this time, but the bullet was wide of the mark and the quartet had already paired off and melted into the shadows of the buildings.

Maguire gave the others time to reach the rear of the now darkened bunk-house before signalling Kermody to move over nearer the house. This way he could draw a bead on the ranch-house itself and fire into the bunk-house.

When Will saw Maguire go down on one knee and throw the carbine to his shoulder, he levered a shell into the breach and sighted on one of the bunk-house windows; one which was half open and from which he believed the second shot had come.

Maguire's rifle cracked and instantly Will let fly at the window. A man's scream rose shrilly into the air and Kermody grinned, guessing that he had winged the man who had been standing by the window searching for a target amongst the shadows.

Almost immediately Herb's rifle kicked up its noise. Like Will's it was one of the new Winchesters and could accurately throw ten .44-.40 shells in ten seconds. The din for a few moments was terrific. Glass shattered, bullets ricocheted off wood or thudded deeply into the log walls, rifles clattered and men's voices were raised sharply, giving instructions. In between whiles Mike Lannigan's Colt did its work.

But now the defenders in the bunk-house were getting the measure of their attackers and both Will and Maguire felt lead scream uncomfortably close as they backed away, half crouched and kept to whatever shadow afforded until reaching a slightly less exposed position.

Suddenly in one of those unaccountable silences, when all noise is curiously suspended at the same psychological moment, Kermody's ear caught the soft sound of sharply moving hoofs, whispering over grassy ground.

Could it be, he wondered, that Mackinnon was indulging in a second run-out on his men that night?

A sudden vision of Ben's treacherous face with its bland and deceptive smile flashed in front of Kermody's eyes. He thought suddenly, *That's Ben escaping, for sure!*

He moved quickly over to Maguire's position and now it seemed that Will had taken charge of the small posse.

'Mackinnon's making a break, Con,' Will said. His words were punched out with an urgent, violent force. 'I'm taking your horse – he's fresh. Am I a deputy or not?'

For a second Maguire gazed into the Stirrup ramrod's hard face and bleak eyes. He did not know the reason for this man's fierce hatred, but he had a shrewd idea. He had seen Kermody's rare concern for Paula Mackinnon after the battle in the Golden Dollar.

He hesitated for a moment only, as these thoughts raced through his mind.

'You're a deputy, Will, an' a dam' good one. Don't go and kill my hoss!'

The Stirrup man was away before Maguire had finished speaking. He shook his head with regret. Regret that for him the blood no longer ran hot and fast in his veins as it did in the young, lithe bodies of men like Will Kermody and Mike Lannigan.

He and Herb Wilson, Con thought, as he turned back to draw a bead on the bunkhouse, were just a couple of ageing law men. They had had their sport and now their lives were a series of rough chores, like this one, with no black-haired woman waiting with open arms!

Will untied Maguire's sturdy paint and vaulted into the saddle, thrusting the Winchester into the boot as he spurred the animal past the house and out onto the range behind.

A shot sailed perilously close and he grinned as he thought of Herb Wilson firing in the belief that this was another Bar 52 rider escaping.

Will found himself on a narrow, natural track that twisted slightly as it unribboned itself across the country. It seemed as good a bet as any that Ben would have started out this way.

In the light cast from the moon Will could see the black masses of timber shouldering their way upwards to the tops of distant hills.

Maybe Ben figured he would have a chance to throw off any pursuit once he could reach the shelter of those blackly wooded slopes.

CHAPTER 17

NO MORE REGRETS!

The firing around the bunk-house at Bar 52 had reduced in intensity since the first ferocious exchanges of shots.

Con Maguire, crouched down behind a stack of driftwood, refilled his empty rifle, speculating on how many of the gunhands inside were hurt and how many would be able to succeed if they chose to make a final dash.

The outbuildings were scattered in random and haphazard fashion and Maguire had no way of knowing, in the darkness, where the corrals and stables were situated.

Once he had essayed a closer inspection, seeking to discover where the horses were, for obvious reasons, but a particularly vicious and well-directed burst of firing had driven him back to the shelter of the wood-pile.

He wondered just what these men expected to get out of it – holding the fort, whilst Mackinnon made his try – and decided that Ben must have emptied a few gold-pokes in order to persuade the men to cover his flight.

Maybe, Con thought, he had even told them some story about going for help...

Maguire threw up his gun suddenly as boots crunched on the gravel nearby.

'*Hold it, Con!*' It was Lannigan's urgent whisper and Maguire eased his finger from the trigger-guard.

'Here!' Maguire called softly and Mike stepped round into the shadows.

'Herb's bin hit,' Lannigan said. 'He ain't dead, but he's passed out. Lost a deal of blood. Where's Will?'

'Taken my horse and ridden out after Mackinnon,' Maguire said. 'Trouble is we can't be in all places at once. We–'

'Listen!' Mike said suddenly, and both men crouched there in silence. Dimly came the sound of hoofbeats from the other side of the buildings.

'Riders comin' in, or–'

Mike shook his head. 'They're breakin' out, Con. C'mon!'

He raced across the yard now, aware that his figure was a target for any guns in the bunk-house, yet no shots came.

He heard the bulky sheriff's laboured running close behind and then the fast rata-plan of racing hoofs swelled to a crescendo as horses were put to the spur.

They broke out of the yard between the nearest outbuildings and the house itself and saw two riders, dim shapes on racing ponies, quartering over towards the distant folds of land.

Lannigan raised his six-gun, sensing the futility of even trying, yet dissatisfied to stand by and do nothing.

Maguire, for all his heavy breathing and the weight he had to carry, threw up his carbine and carefully sighted on the nearest shadowy figure even now almost lost to sight.

His rifle cracked and the rider's horse swerved. As distance lowered its obscuring curtain they saw the small, black figure topple from the saddle and lose itself in the shadows of the range.

'Good shooting, Sheriff!' Lannigan said. 'Reckon we kin find him later. What about tackling the bunk-house?'

Maguire nodded. 'I don't aim to commit suicide,' he said drily, 'but it seems quiet enough now.'

On a sudden thought, Mike halted at the porch of the ranch-house and groped around in the dark, finally risking a match.

As the sulphur flared he found what he had been seeking. A storm lantern. In a moment it was alight, and Mike was carrying it awkwardly in his slinged left hand and partly screening it with his coat.

They cautiously approached nearer to the bunk-house door and nothing stirred. Once they were close to the wall, the first and immediate danger was over.

Maguire paused a moment to listen and then, as though contemptuous of his own actions, suddenly hefted a tremendous kick at the door.

It was hardly surprising that ordinary bolts could not withstand that smashing blow delivered with the full backing of Con Maguire's two hundred and twenty-four pounds.

The door flew open and for perhaps the space of ten seconds they stood quite still.

Somewhere inside a man was moaning softly and then Maguire went in and Mike followed, whipping his coat away from the lantern and gazing down on the scene of carnage.

Three men lay rigid in death, their guns beside them or else clenched in stiffening hands. A fourth man moved feebly as blood gushed from his mouth. It was this one who moaned and Maguire's sober gaze came up to Mike's face.

'Three dead, Lannigan, and that one won't last the night out.'

Mike nodded. 'There were six besides Ben and Art Millar. Four here and the couple who broke out. You got one. That leaves Ben and one other.'

'A fair day's work,' Maguire said, yet though the words sounded flippant, his mood was sober enough.

'You get blankets and cover these men up, Lannigan. I'll go and bring Herb inside. We'll need to dress his wound...'

Kermody studied the country as well as he could from the back of Maguire's flying pony. It was still a long way to dawn and the moon was quartering away to the south-west. The night would grow darker yet before the eastern sky paled to a new day, and Will tried to assess the chances of picking up Mackinnon under these conditions.

There was one thing in his favour and that was the fact that Ben would hardly know this country any better than Will himself. It was doubtful therefore, in making his choice of direction he would have to decide on the more obvious routes.

He would have to keep to what trail there was and be guided by definite landmarks, such as the timbered hills ahead. Otherwise, Will thought, Ben might find himself landing up in a box canyon, or plunging suddenly into a deep arroyo or an unexpected water course.

Thus Will reasoned and spurred the game pony to further efforts, and then Kermody's body stiffened as he glimpsed the small, moving figure ahead, just disappearing over the crest of a ridge.

Now Will applied himself to the chore of getting the maximum effort from Maguire's horse. He shifted his weight slightly in the stirrups and, in the way of a born horseman, communicated his urgent need for speed to the racing animal under him.

Will took the ridge crest in a swirl of dust and a scattering of gravel, glimpsing again the figure ahead and remarking this narrowed distance between himself and Mackinnon.

Whether Ben heard the rataplan of hoofs behind; or whether he was merely making sure of things by occasional backward glances, it was impossible to decide. Sufficient that as Will closed the distance, with the sheriff's pony responding magnificently, Mackinnon took a quick, backward glance and saw the implacable nemesis that was about to overtake him. He could not possibly recognize that darkly crouched figure atop the flying horse, but he knew beyond any doubt that it was Will Kermody and that the sands of time were running out fast.

Will kept both hands on the reins, content to reduce the distance further, content even to allow Ben Mackinnon to make the first aggressive move.

There was the bitter knowledge locked tightly in Kermody's being that for a whole year this man had made Paula Cabot's life unhappy.

That anyone could treat a lovely girl in this fashion was difficult enough to understand. That any man could so use Paula Cabot was utterly incomprehensible to a man of Kermody's sensibilities.

They were now only a bare twenty yards apart and, whilst Maguire's pony was still going strongly, Mackinnon's lathered mount was faltering.

He sensed this and pulled in sharply, and Kermody saw the orange flame blossom in the night as he heard the following roar of the Navy Colt and felt the searing whine of the bullet close to his already scorched cheek. *The second time tonight*, he thought, and raked the pony into a final spurt.

'*Will, Will!*' Mackinnon shouted, his voice rising to the high pitch of near hysteria. '*Don't shoot, Will! I've got the money! I can make you rich…*'

The voice trailed off to a near sob as Kermody pulled his gun from leather and thumbed back the hammer.

Mackinnon's mount was done for now. It had stopped altogether, and as Will sawed on the reins of the sheriff's horse, Ben fired point blank even as he shouted for mercy.

Will felt the stabbing, searing pain in his chest and nausea rose up and filled his mouth and nose.

His reeling brain absorbed the fact that even to the last Mackinnon would be treacherous as any prairie lobo.

Ben's gun rose and lowered again, but even as he fired, Will's savagely triggered shot caught him in the face.

For a moment, in the fading moonlight, Will saw that ghastly, white face, smashed and splotched with ever-thickening blood-stains, and then Ben's massive body swayed and slowly fell from the saddle of the drooping horse.

For a few yards the game beast carried on, dragging Mackinnon's body head first in the dirt, his foot caught in the stirrup. Then, as though the animal sensed that its final efforts had been futile, it stopped short, chest heaving and covered in white sweat, and almost reluctantly, it seemed, Ben's leg fell away from the stirrup and he lay stiff and dark and ugly in death.

Kermody neck-reined his mount, feeling the driving sickness rise up in him and seeing the dark, shadowy country out of focus through pain-filled eyes.

He gripped the saddle-horn with both hands, trusting to the instinct of Maguire's pony to get them back to the Bar 52.

It was a long, grim journey, with the horse walking and Will swaying in the saddle, unable to staunch the flow of blood that slowly saturated his shirt and vest.

An hour, a day, a year later, Kermody neither knew nor cared, he saw the shape of buildings ahead, more clear-cut now that early dawn was lightening the eastern sky.

They were waiting for him in the yard near to the bunk-house, Con Maguire and Mike and Herb with his head bandaged.

Will's face was ugly with pain and dust sprinkled the beard stubble on his sweaty cheeks.

He had fought to keep his weary brain awake, battling against the sea of blanketing fog which had threatened to envelop him.

Vaguely he was aware that these men were his friends and not his enemies, and as they helped him down from the saddle he allowed the flood-tide of blessed unconsciousness to sweep up and over him...

Paula pushed open the screen door and came out on to the gallery as the sun slid down behind the distant Goya range.

She turned towards Will's favourite spot at the end of the gallery, from where he had the greatest unrestricted view of Stirrup land and the snow-capped tips of Spanish Peaks.

He was stretched out in a comfortable chair, his booted feet resting on a stool.

'How do you feel after your first day up, Will?' Paula smiled, seating herself in the vacant chair next to him.

Kermody grinned. 'All I can feel at the moment, Paula, is that I'm dam' lucky to be alive.'

She nodded soberly. 'We didn't think you'd make it, although Doc Laurie said it would take more than a slug in the ribs to finish Will Kermody. But three weeks is a long time, Will!'

'A hell of a long time for a man to sit around doing nothing,' Will said. 'I'm starting in next week with Phil on a chore we've had in mind for some time.'

'You take it easy, boy,' Paula said, and watched the slow smile break up the flat planes of his face. She hadn't called him that for a long time.

'Ward won't be up and about for quite a time,' she said. 'Even when he is up he won't be so active. He wants me to–'

'Boss the spread?' Will asked in shocked dismay. 'Have I got to be bossed by a woman?'

She knew it was only Will's joshing, but somehow that remark had pierced her armour more deeply than many of Ben's cruel thrusts had done in the past.

She got up swiftly and moved to the rail, watching the crimson-and-gold fire of the dying sun set the tips of the Goya range alight.

A rider was coming across the range from the north, which meant, most likely, he was returning from Selwyn.

It was almost dark when Phil Hankins clattered in and drew rein at the gallery.

'Hallo, Miz Paula. Howdy, Will. Heard the news? Celia Owen and Mike Lannigan are getting hitched–'

He stopped short as he caught the look in Paula's eyes. He thought, *You goddam clumsy fool, Hankins, you picked the wrong time!*

The *segundo* turned his horse and murmured, 'Be seein' you,' and swung out in the direction of the corrals.

Behind her Paula heard Will come to his feet but she continued to gaze out across the darkening range.

Someone had lit a lamp in the hallway of the house and the yellow rays streamed out through the wire mesh, forming an open-work pattern of fish-net on the boards of the veranda.

Will's voice came softly across from where he stood in the shadows.

'That makes two, Paula!'

She nodded and replied without turning her head:

'Ray and Laura will make a good team, Will. I'm glad for both their sakes–'

'No regrets at being away from the Golden Dollar?'

Paula turned and faced him now, searching his face for any trace of the banter which she felt had been in his voice.

His face was grave and she knew she was being hypersensitive about all this, yet knowing that she could not help it.

269

'The only regrets I have are that I ever went there, Will. That I ever married Ben. I can no longer feel–'

Will reached her in three strides, catching hold of her upper arms and drawing her closely towards him.

He gazed down into the troubled face and smiled gently. 'You know what's in my mind?' he asked softly.

Paula nodded. 'I – I think so, Will.'

'You figure you might make another mistake – like the last one?'

She nodded miserably and Will pulled her close and kissed her on the lips.

She was trembling when she drew her lips away, moments later.

'Are you still going on thinking of past mistakes or will you take a chance and marry me?'

For a long time she searched his face and slowly the haunted look disappeared from her eyes.

'I think it would be a mistake if I didn't, Will,' she whispered, and raised her lips to his.

The publishers hope that this book has given you enjoyable reading. Large Print Books are especially designed to be as easy to see and hold as possible. If you wish a complete list of our books please ask at your local library or write directly to:

Dales Large Print Books
Magna House, Long Preston,
Skipton, North Yorkshire.
BD23 4ND

This Large Print Book, for people
who cannot read normal print,
is published under the auspices of

THE ULVERSCROFT FOUNDATION

... we hope you have enjoyed this book.
Please think for a moment about those
who have worse eyesight than you ...
and are unable to even read or enjoy
Large Print without great difficulty.

You can help them by sending a
donation, large or small, to:

**The Ulverscroft Foundation,
1, The Green, Bradgate Road,
Anstey, Leicestershire, LE7 7FU,
England.**
or request a copy of our brochure for
more details.

The Foundation will use all donations
to assist those people who are visually
impaired and need special attention
with medical research, diagnosis
and treatment.

Thank you very much for your help.